Under The Mistletoe With Me

A With Me in Seattle Novella

By

Kristen Proby

UNDER THE MISTLETOE WITH ME
A With Me In Seattle Novella
Kristen Proby

Copyright © 2012 by Kristen Proby

Cover image used under license by Foltolia.com
Cover Design by Rachel A. Marks

Dedication:

For Alvin. We know how much work marriage is. Thanks for joining me on the journey. I love you.

Chapter One

"I'm just glad you didn't have a game today and can actually enjoy Thanksgiving dinner with us." My mother-in-law, Gail, smiles over at her son, Will who is currently stuffing his face full of mashed potatoes.

"Me too, Mom. God, this is good."

"That's a lot of carbs for a man in training," Isaac mutters next to me. I run my palm up and down my husband's thigh and grin up at him. He loves giving his brother a hard time.

"Dude, it's Thanksgiving," Will replies.

"So the carbs don't count?" Isaac asks.

"Exactly." Will grins and takes another bite of his potatoes. I am surrounded by a room full of loving, funny people. The Montgomery gene pool is impressive. But more than being, well, gorgeous, they are welcoming and good-hearted, and I'm proud and lucky to be a part of them.

Sophie, our four-month-old daughter, squirms in my arms.

"Here, babe, let me take her." Isaac pulls our baby girl into his arms and lays her on his broad shoulder. She settles in and falls back to sleep, her face pressed against his neck. I can't blame her, it's one my favorite places to be too. "You eat, honey."

We are all gathered at Luke and Natalie's house for the holiday. The loving couple have been married for about two months now, and I couldn't be happier for them. Natalie isn't a sister by blood, but she's been a part of this family for years. She and Jules', the youngest and only girl of the Montgomery clan, are the best of friends. With the addition of Luke's parents, Lucy and Neil, and two siblings, Samantha and Mark, along with my parents as well, this house is overflowing with bodies, loud with voices and laughter, and is a little too warm.

There is no where I'd rather be.

"Stace, how is your blog going?" Jules asks next to me.

"It's going well, thanks. I really love it."

"She's being modest," Isaac cuts in with a grin. "It's going great. She's got over two thousand followers, and her reviews have been picked up by some publishers to add to book covers."

He smiles down at me and kisses my forehead, his blue eyes shining with pride. *God, I love him.*

"What kind of books are you reviewing?" Natalie asks.

"Romance novels," I reply with a smile.

"The dirty kind?" Will asks hopefully, earning a smack in the arm from Luke's sister, Samantha. "What?"

"Don't be a perv," she mutters, glaring at him.

"Actually, all kinds, but yes, the erotic novels are pretty hot right now," I respond and wink at him.

"Oh! Have you read those books that everyone's been talking about?" Samantha asks. "You know, the ones where the guy ties her up and spanks her and is all kinds of naughty?"

I feel my ears burn as I blush. The guys all roll their eyes, but Matt, Isaac's younger brother, clears his throat and won't look anyone in the eye.

Interesting.

"Yes, I've read them, Sam."

"I could use some of those," Jules whispers in my ear. "I've hit a dry spell."

"I'll email you a list," I whisper back and we giggle.

"What are you whispering about?" Isaac asks, pulling my hand up to kiss my knuckles.

"Just books," I reply.

"Okay, gimme the baby." Natalie stands and walks around the table, her arms open, and scoops Sophie up off of Isaac's shoulder, nuzzling her. "Hi, precious. I missed you."

My gaze finds Luke. He's watching his wife, his blue eyes full of love and contentment. Natalie is pregnant herself.

"Anytime you want practice with middle of the night feedings, you're welcome to it," Isaac tells her.

I roll my eyes and smack his arm. "Quit trying to give my baby away."

He winks at me and takes a bite of his turkey. "I'm just kidding."

"You know I'd keep her in a heartbeat," Natalie responds with a happy smile and kisses Sophie's cheek, making her giggle.

Isaac's phone rings in his pocket. He checks the display and scoots his chair back.

"I'll be right back."

I wonder who it could be? Surely not work on Thanksgiving. I shrug it off and finish my dinner, and then help clear the table and clean the kitchen. With all of us chipping in, the chores are done quickly and we all settle in with glasses of wine or coffee to chat and recover from the delicious Thanksgiving meal.

Finally, Isaac returns from his phone call, a frown on his handsome face. "Who was that?"

"It was nothing." He shakes his head and walks to the kitchen to pull a beer out of the fridge before sitting next to me on the couch.

"It was some*one*," I respond.

He shakes his head again and takes a pull from his beer. "Don't worry about it."

I frown up at him. This is new. It's not that we have to share every little detail about who we talk to, but we usually do. He's never been evasive before.

Before I can argue with him, he takes my hand in his and links our fingers, bringing them up to his lips. "Just drop it."

He grins down at me and winks, then strikes up a conversation with Will about his football season with the Seahawks, effectively closing the subject. With a full belly, and a warm fire blazing not far away, I settle in next to my firm husband, rest my head on his muscular shoulder, and watch the activity around me.

"Stacy, here are the photos we took last week of Sophie," Natalie hands me a thumb drive. "I think you'll like them."

"Oh, I know I'll love them! Thanks again for doing it. I'll order Christmas cards next week." I grin at her as she takes a seat across from me with Jules.

Jules and Nat have their heads together, as usual, cooing over a sleeping Sophie. I smile at the three of them. Three beautiful girls. I pull my phone out of my pocket and snap a photo of them.

Sam sits next to them and kisses Sophie's head, and I snap another photo.

All of our parents are settled around the dining room table with coffee, chatting about grandkids and Christmas plans.

Will and Isaac ramble on about football, with Matt, their other brother, and Luke chiming in here and there. Mark saunters in from the kitchen, passes Luke another beer and joins them. The only one missing is Caleb, who is off on some SEAL mission.

I hope he'll be home for Christmas.

"You okay?" Isaac whispers.

"Mmm."

He grins down at me and kisses my hair. My eyes are heavy. I let my eyelids fall and listen to the conversations around me.

"I'll be back in a minute." Isaac catches my chin in his fingers and kisses me softly. I never get tired of his lips. My man can kiss. He moves away from me and lowers me onto the couch so my head is on the armrest and I feel him walk away from me.

Will, Luke and Mark are enthralled in football talk, passionately arguing about the offensive line.

Suddenly, my eyes blink open and I wonder how long I've slept. I didn't mean to drift off.

Our moms have left their husbands at the table and joined the rest of us girls in the living room. My mom cradles Sophie in her arms, earning a frown from Jules.

"I never get to hold her. Between Natalie and you guys, I never get her."

"Don't whine," Natalie mutters.

"Shut up," Jules responds, and I giggle. They are so funny, even when they bicker.

"Stace, I'm glad the blog is going well," Luke's mom Lucy says with a smile.

"Thanks, me too. I just need something to do while I'm home with Sophie. Don't get me wrong, I'm not bored, but I just…" How do I explain that I need something, just for me, without sounding selfish?

"I get it," Lucy responds.

"So, let's talk strategy, girls." Jules rubs her hands together and perches at the edge of the couch with a large stack of newspaper ads. "Black Friday." She grins excitedly and bounces on the cushion, her pretty blonde hair bouncing with her, licks her finger and grabs the ad on top, flipping through it.

"I'm not going at 4:00 am this time," Natalie informs her while she rubs her tiny baby bump. "This little one won't let me out of bed that early."

"I can't do that early either," I chime in.

"I'm doing my shopping online." Sam waves us off and rolls her eyes. "I refuse to get into a fist fight over a scarf."

"You're no fun," Jules pouts.

"I'm in, if we leave around seven. I can have Sophie fed and be ready myself."

"Okay, Nat and I will pick you up then."

"Gonna spend all my money, baby?" Luke murmurs into Nat's ear as she climbs into his lap. He wraps his arms around her and holds her close and I can't help but grin at them. They are so in love.

"Yep. All of it. We'll be homeless when I'm done."

"It's okay, we'll go live with Jules."

"Oh hell no." Jules shakes her head and laughs. "We'll save enough money for you to cover the mortgage."

"Oh good," he replies dryly.

"Well, some of us *are* on a budget," I inform them with a chuckle. "So go easy on me."

"It's gonna be so fun!" Jules claps her hands as Sophie begins to fuss in my mom's arms.

"We should probably head home," I murmur and stand, stretching my arms up over my head. "Will, where are Isaac and Matt?"

"I think they're on the deck." Will responds, and then returns to his football conversation with the boys.

What is it with men and football?

I walk over to the patio door and open it quietly. I hear my husband's deep voice say, "I just don't know what to do about her."

"Well, bro.." Matt begins but stops when he sees me in the doorway. He offers me a smile. "Hey, Stace."

"Hey." I step out on the deck and smile at Isaac, but my stomach is in knots as I remember the mysterious phone call at dinner, and now this. "What's going on?"

Isaac shakes his head and shrugs nonchalantly. "Nothing."

"Uh, huh." I eye him, knowing he's keeping something from me, but then I hear Sophie cry inside. "We should go. Soph is ready for bed."

"Okay, let's go."

Chapter Two

"Are you sure you don't want me to take Soph to my mom's?" I ask Isaac as I bustle around the kitchen, putting breakfast supplies away.

"Nah, we'll be fine." He cradles her against his chest, bouncing her slightly and smiles at me. "Have fun today. Don't worry about us."

"I intend to have fun. And shop my ass off. I am bringing a change of socks to refresh my feet half way through."

Isaac shakes his head and laughs. "I don't get Black Friday."

"It's a challenge that involves shopping. It's not for you to understand." I switch my phone to vibrate and shove it in my pocket, throw my keys in my purse and glance up at my husband. "Hey, question."

"Okay."

"What was going on last night at Luke and Nat's?"

Isaac frowns and sighs. "Stace, don't worry about it. Have fun today, and we'll talk later."

"We don't keep secrets."

"I'm not keeping one now. I want you to have fun today. We'll talk later."

"If you say so." He leans down and kisses me chastely, then grips my jaw in his hand and deepens the kiss, making my toes curl. He smells like coffee, his body wash and just Isaac, and when he pulls back and gives me that cocky grin with his bright blue eyes smiling at me, I can't help but sigh, even after being with him all these years.

"I'll see you later," I whisper when I hear Jules honk her horn outside.

"Be safe." He kisses my forehead. I lean in to kiss Sophie's cheek and I'm out the door.

***

Sometimes, you just need a day out with the girls, and I've realized today that it's been far too long since I've taken time away from the baby to just enjoy my friends. We have been all over Seattle, following sales and just enjoying each other's company.

"You scored on that watch for Will at Macy's." Jules comments as she holds a sweater up.

"I know, I hope he likes it."

"He will. Besides that man needs a watch. He's always late."

My phone vibrates in my pocket and I pull it out to check the text.

nipples.

Huh? Isaac has sent me a text that just says *nipples*? Is he talking about nipples for Sophie's bottle?

"Oh, look! The baby section. C'mon, guys, I wanna look." Natalie leads us to the brightly colored baby section to look through clothes and other gear.

My phone vibrates again.

I luv it when u ride me and I can play with ur

My husband has lost his mind. Or someone has stolen his phone and is sending me obscene text messages.

I vaguely hear Jules and Nat chattering around me, but I'm not paying attention to what they're saying or even what they're looking at. I'm just mindlessly following them through the store, winding through clothes racks and around a loud Santa and elves and kids yelling and crying.

It's really, really loud in here.

nd cum in ur mouth.

What the hell? I stare down at my phone and frown.

"Oh, Stace, Sophie would be so cute in this!"

I tuck my phone in my pocket and look over at Jules holding up an adorable black romper. "Oh, that's adorable! I'll take it."

My phone vibrates again, so I pull it out and check the text.

You make me so hard.

Isaac hasn't talked to me like this in years. *Years.* Before I can shove my phone back in my pocket, it vibes again and another text from him pops on the screen.

I want u kneeling in front of me with ur pretty pink lips around my cock. I'm gonna pull your hair a

That's it. The last of the text is cut off again. This isn't *my* husband. We haven't done the dirty talk thing since before Sophie was born. Hell, since before Sophie was conceived.

"Stacy?" I hear Nat calling my name, but before I can answer, one more text comes through.

This is what I'm gonna give you 2nite. Be ready. And… it's a picture of his dick.

"Stacy?" Jules lays her hand on my arm to get my attention, and I meet her concerned blue gaze with my own.

"What the fuck is up with your brother?"

"What are you talking about?" Jules asks.

"He's sending me obscene text messages, which I'm starting to think aren't intended for me, given that he hasn't talked dirty to me like this in years, and last night at Nat's he took a *private* call that he won't tell me about and was talking about some woman with Matt. Jules, if your brother is fucking around on me, so help me God…"

Jules laughs and shakes her head. "Stacy, you know he's not fucking around."

"As of right this minute, I'm not so sure."

And the magnitude of that statement paralyzes me. I stare at my friends and replay last night and this morning in my head, his evasiveness, telling me to drop it, but kissing me to cover it up. I feel my eyes widen and my heart rate triples.

"Fuck."

"Stacy, I'm sure there's an explanation. Isaac is nuts about you." Natalie rubs my back in large circles, trying to console me.

"He is, Stace." Jules nods. "I know he loves you and Sophie more than anything."

"That doesn't mean that he's not having an affair," I whisper.

"C'mon, let's get out of here. I think we've done enough damage to my credit card for one day." Jules sets the few things we'd picked up on a rack and we walk through the store and out to the car.

"I don't understand what's happening," I whisper.

"Well, your first step is to talk to him. Ask him." Natalie says from the back seat behind me. Jules is driving, where I don't know, and I'm in the passenger seat.

"I did ask him. He told me to drop it. This morning he told me to have fun today and we'd talk tonight. Oh, God, he's going to tell me he's leaving me." My stomach convulses and I start to pant.

"Stacy, don't be dramatic." Jules rolls her eyes and merges into traffic, heading toward my house.

"Where are we going?"

"We're going to your place."

"I don't want to see Isaac yet. I need to calm down and think."

"No, you need to confront my brother and find out what the hell he's doing."

I twist my fingers in my lap and bite my lip until it bleeds. "Maybe you can confront him and let me know how it goes."

"Oh no, this is all you. But if you want us there with you, we'll stay. Are you afraid of him?" She looks over to me with narrowed eyes.

"No! No, I'm not afraid of him, I just don't know if I want the answer to my questions."

"Stacy, I'm telling you," Natalie says firmly. "Isaac is not fucking around."

"I wouldn't have ever expected him to." My God, we've had ups and downs, but never, *never* would I have suspected that he could ever do this to me.

"So, to recap," Jules starts as she pulls into my driveway, "He took a mysterious phone call at Nat's last night that he doesn't want to talk about, and today he sent you dirty texts."

"Yes."

"This does not make for an affair, Stace."

"I know, but it's so not him."

"There are no photos of naked women, you haven't caught him in bed with anyone…"

"No."

Jesus, I'd die if I found him in bed with another woman. Correction: the other woman would die. A slow, painful death.

"I think this is a misunderstanding," Natalie says gently. "But, where is this insecurity in your marriage coming from? This isn't like you, honey. You are not this insecure."

"I know." I bite my lip again and fight tears. I haven't felt like myself since the baby came. Our marriage hasn't felt the same. "Since the baby was born, our sex life hasn't been the greatest. We're both really tired all the time." I shrug and look down at my hands in embarrassment. "I know our marriage isn't perfect, but I've never felt this disconnected from him. If I'm not satisfying him, someone else will. You've seen him."

"Oh, for the love of Moses, Stacy, listen to yourself. I think you need some hot sex and a vacation, girl," Jules comments, making me laugh.

"Yeah, that couldn't hurt."

Isaac's truck is in the driveway of our pretty two-story home. It occurs to me that he put the Christmas lights up today, which just makes me more emotional. This is Sophie's first Christmas. What if we don't get to spend it as a family in our home?

Jules cuts the engine and pops the trunk.

"C'mon, let's get your stuff inside."

We carry my plethora of bags full of gifts for the whole family, and way more than Sophie will ever need or remember for her first Christmas, into the house. Isaac is packing a diaper bag and has the car seat by the door.

"Ladies, you're back sooner than I expected." He flashes us a wide happy smile, but all I see is the bag he's packing.

"Where the hell are you going?" I ask. I hear the desperation in my voice, I know I sound like a complete lunatic, but I can't make it stop.

"Uh," He frowns at me and pushes his hand through his soft, dark blonde hair. "Nowhere. I was going to ask Jules if she would take Sophie home with her for a few hours so you and I can have some alone time."

"Of course I'll take Sophie!" Jules says from behind me. "Nat, will you help Isaac finish loading the baby's bag while I help Stacy upstairs with her stuff?"

"On it."

Isaac looks at the three of us like we've lost our minds. "What's going on?"

Jules just leads me up the stairs as I hear Natalie say, "You guys really need to talk, you dumb ass."

Chapter Three

"So, talk to me." Isaac walks into our bedroom and crosses to me, planting his hands on his lean hips. Jules and Nat just left with Sophie and we're all alone.

"No, you start talking. I want to know who you were talking to last night. And who the hell did you intend to send those text messages to today?"

Yes, I sound like a nagging, bitchy wife, but I can't stop it. I pull my coat off with jerking movements and throw it on top of the bags on our bed and turn back around to face him, crossing my arms over my chest.

"Stacy, what are you accusing me of?" he asks in a low voice, his blue eyes narrowed.

"I'm not accusing, I'm asking. Again. I've been asking since last night."

"I spoke to Brynna last night at Luke's, Stacy. She was in trouble and is on her way here."

What? Brynna is my cousin, but we were raised as sisters.

"She's on her way from Chicago?"

"Yes."

"But the kids…"

"Are with her."

"Is she driving?"

"Yes."

"What the hell, Isaac? Why didn't you tell me this last night?"

"Because I didn't want to worry you. It was Soph's first Thanksgiving, and Matt and I have it taken care of." He runs his hands through his hair and paces away from me toward the bathroom.

"Why is she coming here?"

"I don't know all the details yet, I just know that she was scared and said she needed to get out of there fast and was heading here."

I just stand and blink at him. Brynna, the person I'm closest to in the world, is coming home and is in trouble and I'm just now finding out?

"Isaac..."

"Yeah, I know, in hindsight I probably should have said something, but you would have worried, and I wanted you to enjoy the holiday."

Okay.

"Where is she now?"

"I'm not sure, she's taking it slow because of the weather and the kids, but she should be here by the middle of next week. Matt's keeping close tabs on her."

Isaac's brother Matt is a Seattle cop, and I know he'll do everything in his power to help Brynna. The Montgomery men take care of their family, and because of me, Brynna is family too, so I trust that she'll be safe.

"Now, about the texts," Isaac mumbles and my anger sparks again. "Let me see your phone." He holds his large hand out expectantly.

"Why? So you can delete them?"

"Jesus, Stacy, what is wrong with you? Just give me your phone, please." He appears exasperated and worried, but not like he's feeling guilty, which gives me hope, so I hand him my phone. He locates the texts and frowns as he reads through them.

"You got them all out of order."

"You think?"

"I hate being on two different cell services."

"Isaac, I don't think the fact that we have two different plans is the point right now. Who did you intend to send those to?"

"You." He passes the phone back to me with a frown. "Who else would I send sexy messages to?"

"You tell me."

"What has gotten into you? I just wanted to send you some fun texts to spice things up a bit. I'm fucking flirting with my wife, that's all!" Now he's pissed; fiery blue eyes, jaw set in a grim line, hands back on his hips.

I feel like a complete idiot. I close my eyes and sit on the edge of the bed, lowering my head and bracing my face in my hands.

What is wrong with me?

"Baby, talk to me." Isaac kneels in front of me and pulls my hands away from my face. He cups my cheek in his hand, brushing his thumb along my skin and I feel tears well in my eyes.

"I thought…"

"I know what you thought, and it pisses me the hell off, but tell me why you went there, Stace. This isn't who we are."

I close my eyes again as relief surges through me and I grip his wrist with my hand, keeping his hand against my cheek.

"Since Sophie was born, we seem different," I whisper and open my eyes. "We're so busy with her, you with the company, and me with the blog, and we're always so damn tired. I just miss you. And I know that we don't make love like we used to, and well…"

"You assumed I'd go looking for it somewhere else."

It's not a question. I cringe at the cold edge of his voice and focus down at his chest.

"I've never given you a reason to believe that, Stacy." God, he sounds angry, and I can't blame him.

"You're right, and I'm sorry. But you seemed to be hiding something from me, and the texts were a shock. You haven't flirted with me like that since long before the baby."

"I know." He runs his fingers down my cheek before gripping my hands tightly in his. I love how big and strong his hands are. "When we were in Tahiti for the wedding, you were so relaxed and fun, and I realized that I miss you too, babe. The sex was great, and we laughed like we haven't in a long time. It's time to reconnect. I want to start dating again."

"Dating?" I giggle.

"Well, yeah. I want to do things with just the two of us. It doesn't have to be all the time, because Sophie is part of us, but we have a huge family who would love nothing more than to keep her once in a while, so I say we take advantage of it and spend some time together."

And I melt. This is exactly what we need, what I've been missing.

"We only leave her with family," I reply sternly.

"Of course, I wouldn't leave her with just anyone. But you know our parents would love to spend extra time with her every few weeks or so."

He's right, they would, but it'll be hard to be away from her. Yet, mending the connection between Isaac and me is imperative.

"You're right. How should we start?" I ask.

"Well, right now…" he gives me that smile, the one he uses when he's seducing me, and damned if it doesn't always work.

"Right now?" I whisper.

He leans in and lightly brushes his lips across mine, once, then again, nibbling lightly at the edges of my lips.

"Right." Kiss. "Now."

Oh, hell yes.

He pulls me to my feet and yanks my blue long-sleeved t-shirt over my head, then pulls his own gray tee off and throws them aside. While I make quick work of my jeans and underwear, he swipes his hands over the bed, sending bags and boxes to the floor.

"I hope there wasn't anything fragile in there," he remarks with a grin and I shake my head, smiling back at him. His blue eyes light up at the sight of me naked, and he pulls me close, wrapping his arms around my waist and holding me firmly against him. "Did you eat lunch?"

Lunch?

"Uh, yeah."

"Good, you're going to need the energy." He buries his face in my neck, nibbling and sucking his way up to my ear and across my jawline. I reach for his jeans and unfasten them, slide my hands between his boxer-briefs and skin, and push them over his hips and down his legs, kissing his chest and sculpted abdomen.

His erection is full and hard, and without touching it with my hands, I circle my tongue around the tip. Isaac gasps, sucking air in through his teeth and I grin as I stand back up.

"God, I want you." His eyes travel from my face down my body, over my breasts, my stomach, legs and back up again and I return the favor, taking in his amazing body. Working construction for almost fifteen years has kept him in fantastic shape, his muscles tight and firm. His skin is still bronze from our trip to Tahiti. He's clean shaven, but he needs a haircut. His dark blonde hair is wavy, and unruly from running his fingers through it. Mine are itching to get into it too.

But it's his Montgomery blue eyes that have always captivated me, that prompted my nickname *Eyes* for him, a variation of his name, and those incredibly blue eyes. They're smiling at me now, hot and full of promise and lust and if my panties were still on they'd be soaked.

He takes my hand and pulls me flush against him, links our fingers and rests our hands at the small of my back. I trace his chin with my nose, and push the fingers of my free hand through his soft hair.

"Stace," he whispers. I gaze into his eyes as he gently kisses my lips.

"Yeah?"

"If you ever even think about me fucking around on you again," he mutters, deceptively softly, against my lips, "I will spank the living shit out of you."

My eyes go wide and I gape at him. Holy shit, this is new.

"Okay." *How the hell do I respond to that?*

"I'm not kidding." He pulls his fingers down my face, down my neck and cups my breast in his palm, worrying the tight nipple in his fingers. My head falls back and I bite my lip. "I haven't looked at another woman in ten years." His lips skim down my neck, and finally he cups my ass in his hands and lifts me, pivots, and lays me back on the bed. He crawls over me and rests his hard cock against my pussy while his mouth does incredibly naughty things to mine.

His tongue is strong and sure, insistent, dancing against my own. His elbows are planted on the bed at either side of my head and his fingers are buried in my hair. I run my hands down his smooth back to his ass and back up again. I love the feel of him. It never gets old.

I roll my hips, and gasp as the tip of his cock brushes against my clit.

"Ah, baby, you're so wet," he murmurs against my mouth and pulls back to rest his swollen head against my labia. I press my feet against his ass, urging him inside.

"I want you."

With a growl he pushes inside me, burying himself to the root, and rests his forehead against mine. I gasp at the intrusion, my body still unused to making love after giving birth to our daughter, but he stills and lets me acclimate to him and the tiny pain subsides.

"You feel so good."

"I've been doing my kegels."

"Gazoontite."

I burst out laughing, tightening around him, making him moan. "It means I'm exercising the muscles down there to tighten them back up from the pregnancy."

"I know, I just love it when you laugh when I'm inside you."

I grin up at him and take his face in my palms. "I love you, Eyes."

He crushes his mouth to mine and moves faster, harder, grinding his pelvis against my clit with every stroke in and I feel the building inside me begin, my muscles tighten, my thighs clench. I grip his hair in my fingers and throw my head back as I come around him, surprised at how strong my orgasm is, and so happy that my body is starting to feel back to normal again.

"That's right, baby, I wanna feel you come on my cock."

"Shit!" I wrap my legs more tightly around his hips as I spasm around him, and I feel his own orgasm work its way through him. He thrusts once, then again and grinds into me forcefully, spilling himself inside me.

He collapses over me with a big sigh, rests his cheek on my shoulder and murmurs, "Only you, babe."

***

I wake alone, disoriented. There's a full moon shining brightly, illuminating the room. The bed is cold where Isaac was asleep a few hours ago and the house feels still.

I rise from the bed, stretching my arms over my head, feeling the pull of muscles well used this afternoon from our unexpected and hot lovemaking. I grin and push my hair back from my face. Perhaps we need an encore.

I wonder where he is.

I pad quietly down the dark hallway, expecting to go downstairs and find him in the kitchen, but as I pass Sophie's room, I hear Isaac's voice, speaking in hushed tones. The dim light on the dresser is on, sending a shadow across the hallway floor. I peek in, to see Isaac rocking gently in the lovely, plush sage-colored rocking chair he got me when I was pregnant. Sophie is resting in the crook of his elbow, suckling a bottle, her big blue eyes watching her daddy's face.

God, I love them.

Isaac brushes his hand gently over her little head and smiles down at his daughter.

"You're as pretty as your mommy, you know. I hope you get her hair. I love the color of her hair." He's whispering down at her, like they're having a deep conversation, and Soph's eyes are pinned to his, listening while she eats.

"You have her temper too, don't you?" I grin to myself and lean my forehead against the door frame, listening out of sight. "That's okay, it just means that you know what you want. You'll give some poor bastard a run for his money. But not until your forty."

Sophie sighs. "Okay, burp time, baby girl." I hear rustling as he settles her on his shoulder to pat her back. "What should we get mommy for Christmas?"

As much as I really, really want to stand and eaves drop, I decide I've heard enough and walk into the room. God, she looks so small against his wide shoulder and with his big hand on her back. He glances up and grins at me.

"Did I wake you?"

"No, I woke and you were gone, so I thought I'd come find you." I kiss Sophie's soft head and inhale her baby smell and then lean over and kiss my sweet husband's lips.

"Her highness was hungry."

"So I see," I reply with a chuckle. "You're so good with her."

"I hope so, she's stuck with me."

"Yeah, that's not such a bad deal." Sophie has fallen back to sleep. "Let's put her back down and go back to bed, Eyes."

He smiles. "That's the best offer I've had all day."

Chapter Four

"Why in the name of all that's holy is it always so much colder at Christmas tree farms than it is anywhere else? Do they secretly have A/C piped in vents under the trees or something? Because I swear to God, it was not this cold at home." I shift side to side, trying to keep warm and lift the blanket I have covering Sophie to check on her. She's snuggled in her sling across my chest, warm as can be, sleeping soundly.

At least one of us is warm.

"I know how to warm you up, baby." Isaac winks at me and flashes a wolfish grin and I can't help but laugh.

"Yes, I'm aware, but I'm not taking my clothes off out here, buddy. So which one do we want?"

We are wandering around a tree farm, Isaac with axe in-hand, trying to find our Christmas tree. I'm not exactly sure why we're getting a real tree, especially one we have to cut down ourselves, when I have a perfectly good fake tree in a box at home.

Isaac thinks that Sophie needs a real tree for her first Christmas.

"You know, Sophie isn't going to remember this tree, Isaac. The fake tree would be fine."

He turns to glare at me. "I've let you put that ugly ass fake tree up for the past eight years. We are getting a real tree this year."

"What if we get it home and it has spiders in it? Or a squirrel?" I bite my lower lip, trying to keep my smile at bay.

I love irritating him.

"This is not *National Lampoon's Christmas Vacation.*"

"Oh, I'm so relieved."

"You're a smart ass today," he mutters as he continues to peruse through the trees.

"I'm cold. If I keep talking my lips won't freeze shut."

Suddenly, Isaac's gloved hand grips the back of my head and pulls me to him. His lips claim mine, and he kisses me long and slow, his tongue tracing my lips and then tangling with my own. He nibbles the side of my mouth, rubs his cold nose against mine and sinks into me again, his lips soft and lazy. Finally he pulls back, his blue eyes shining, and exhales.

"Lips warmer?"

"Yes, thanks." I'm struck speechless. Wow.

"Good. Let's find Sophie's tree."

"This is a nice one," he points to a large, full, tall evergreen.

"It's way too tall."

He eyes me speculatively, like I'm deliberately raining on his parade and I giggle as he reaches for his tape measure.

"Damn it," he mutters and looks to the next tree.

Finally, we find the perfect tree and Isaac quickly chops it down, yelling "Timber!" as it falls to the ground.

"You've always wanted to do that, haven't you?" I ask.

He laughs. "Yeah."

He grips the freshly cut trunk and lifts it, ready to pull it behind him as we make our way back to the truck. On the way out, we stop by the farm store and buy some fresh garland, a wreath for the front door and poinsettias.

Isaac grabs some mistletoe and throws it on the pile and winks at me. "I love getting you under the mistletoe, baby."

"Yeah?"

He grins again.

"You don't need mistletoe for that."

"It doesn't hurt."

Our house is going to be very festive this year.

***

"So, where are you?" I ask Brynna and glance around the pub from my corner table. Isaac asked me to meet him here when he got off work for drinks, thus beginning our new dating life, and I'm excited to see him.

"We're somewhere in nowhere North Dakota," Brynna responds dryly.

"How has the weather been?" I ask.

"Shitty. That's why we're in nowhere North Dakota. We're taking it slow. I'm in no huge hurry, other than we're running out of clean clothes and the kids are restless so I can't drive as many hours of the day as I'd like."

"I'm sorry, Bryn. What happened?"

"I'll tell you about it when I get there," she responds with a sigh. "There are listening ears in the backseat."

"Okay." My really cute, young, and possibly working his way through until his modeling career picks up waiter brings me my drink and winks at me.

"Thanks," I mouth at him.

"No problem. I'll check on you in a minute."

The margarita is cold and tart and that first sip is heaven.

"How are you and Isaac doing? Any better?" she asks. I've confided in Brynna about the recent distance between Isaac and me. She's the only person I'd confide everything in.

"We are doing better. As a matter of fact, I'm sitting in a bar waiting for him to meet me. We're dating."

"Dating?" she asks with a laugh. "Where's Sophie?"

"With Isaac's parents. They were thrilled to take her for a few hours. I'm getting used to that part. I text poor Gail like crazy."

"I bet."

"And let me tell you, the sex has been fantastic."

"Well at least one of us is getting some. Good for you guys, girl. I'm so glad it's going better."

"Me too, thanks."

"Okay, well, our rest stop is over, so I'm going to get back on the road. I'll be in touch."

"Okay, sweetie, drive safely. Love you."

"Love you too. Bye."

I set my phone on the table and look up as my adorable waiter has a seat across from me.

"Hi there, beautiful."

"Uh, hi. Can I help you?"

He laughs and sips on a glass of water he's brought with him. "I just thought I'd spend my break time with a gorgeous woman."

What the hell?

"I'm Scott," he continues and holds his hand out for me to shake.

"Stacy," I respond and shake his hand.

"Great name." He flashes another smile, and I see two deep dimples wink at me from each cheek.

He's adorable.

What is he doing here?

"So, why are you here alone?"

"She's not."

We both turn our heads at Isaac's cold voice. He's glaring at the poor kid.

"Oh, sorry man, didn't know she was taken."

"Right. The wedding ring wasn't a clue?" Isaac asks sarcastically, not taking his intimidating gaze away from Scott's face as he hastily climbs off the stool.

"I was too blinded by those amazing hazel eyes and wavy auburn hair to notice her hands, bro. You're a lucky guy." He winks at me, grabs his water and is gone, leaving me with my mouth hanging open.

Isaac takes the seat Scott just vacated and glares over at me.

"What did I do?" I ask innocently.

"Do you have to make yourself look that good in public?" He's dead serious.

I glance down at my white button-down blouse and dark denim jeans.

"I'm not dressed up," I reply.

"You don't have to get dressed up. Now that you're not pregnant anymore, I'm gonna have to kick ass again." His eyes soften and he takes my hand in his, linking our fingers.

"Yeah, right." I laugh and toss my hair over my shoulder. "Besides, you didn't have anything to worry about. That kid was way too young for me."

"He was old enough."

I glance over toward the bar where Scott is standing, talking to the bartender, and he smiles over at me again, his dimples winking in his cheeks.

Holy hotness.

Isaac sighs and I glance back over at him. His eyes are narrowed on my face. His too-long hair is brushed back and disorderly from his fingers. He's all broad shoulders and tanned skin and sexy blue eyes.

"I prefer men over boys." I grin at him and take a sip of my margarita. "I especially prefer the man I'm looking at right now."

He smiles and kisses my fingers. "That's better."

"Would you like a drink?" I start to signal for the waiter, but he stops me.

"No, we're not staying."

"We're not?"

He flashes me that cocky grin and shakes his head. "Nope."

"Where are we going?"

"I have a surprise for you. We're going away for a couple days."

My eyebrows climb into my hairline and my jaw drops. "*Days?* Have you forgotten that we have an infant?"

"Of course not," he frowns at me and links our hands together. "My parents are going to keep her."

"Isaac…"

"She'll be fine. We're not going far. We can be home in the blink of an eye if need be."

Leave Sophie for a couple of days?

"Is there cell reception where we're going?"

"Yes, and wifi. We can be in constant contact if need be." He kisses my fingers. "I'll miss her too, baby, but I really think we need this."

"But, you have work. It's the middle of the week."

"Babe, we own the company. I can take all the time off I want. And I want to spend a few days alone with my gorgeous hazel-eyed, wavy auburn-haired wife." He winks and I laugh loudly.

"You're such a smart ass."

"It's the truth. The kid has good taste. I might have to kill him, but he has good taste." He shrugs and grins.

Wow.

"A few days?" I ask weakly.

"Yes."

"Where are we going?" I ask and finish my margarita.

"You'll see when we get there."

***

'There' is a cabin on a lake about an hour outside of Seattle. Actually, to be more accurate, it's a huge two-story log home nestled in tall evergreens, hidden on the shore of a large, breathtaking lake.

The house has a deck on the upper floor, facing the water, complete with a hot tub. It has a wide open floor plan with cathedral ceilings in the living area, modern gourmet kitchen with stainless steel appliances and brown granite countertops, and three large bedrooms upstairs with en suite bathrooms.

It's incredible.

"You rented this whole house for just the two of us?" I ask.

"Yeah. A hotel isn't private enough, and I wanted to be close to home in case Sophie needed us. A colleague owns this place."

"It's great." I smile over at him as he wheels our suitcase behind him. A suitcase I didn't even know he'd packed.

"It is." He grins back down at me. "The kitchen is stocked in case you're hungry. I'm going to start a fire."

"That sounds good. Are you hungry? I can make us some dinner."

"Yes, please."

I cross to the kitchen and start looking through the fridge and pantry, deciding what to whip up for dinner. This kitchen is amazing. "Who stocked this?" I ask.

"I don't know, Ben said he'd take care of it."

"Ben?"

"The owner."

I find a bunch of fruit, cheeses, sliced meat and crackers and pile it all on a plate. There is also a bottle of good white wine chilling in the fridge, so I pull that out, uncork it and pour us each a glass. Gathering the glasses and plate, I join Isaac by the fire. We curl up at opposite ends of the couch, the plate between us, and nibble, watching the flames dance in the fireplace.

I check my phone for any Sophie updates and smile at the photo of Sophie taking a bath in Gail's kitchen sink, then put it on the coffee table.

"This was a good idea," I sigh and rest my cheek on the back of the couch, facing my impressive husband. He flashes his smile and nods.

"I'm glad you think so. I was afraid you wouldn't want to leave Soph overnight."

"It was really, really hard, but she's in capable hands. I'll just call and check up on her a few thousand times."

He chuckles and removes the plate from the couch, placing it on the floor, and pulls me to him, cradling me between his legs, with my head on his chest. I bury my nose between his pecs and take a deep breath. He smells of fresh laundry and my husband. I feel him rest his lips on the crown of my head and he runs his hands down my back.

"It's supposed to snow," I murmur and feel him smile.

"They always say that, but it rarely happens. This is Seattle." He brushes his hands through my thick hair and I sigh. When was the last time we were able to do this? Just be us, without any interruptions?

I don't remember.

"How's work been?" I ask.

"Busy, but good. I haven't been able to work in the field as much as I like. Too many phone calls and desk work to get done."

"That's what happens when you're the boss."

"I think I'll hire more office help so I can be out with the guys more."

"That sounds good." Isaac grips my chin and tilts my head back to look up at him.

"How are you feeling?" he asks, making me smile.

"I'm good. Hormones are finally starting to stabilize."

He chuckles. "Thank God."

"I wasn't that bad." I murmur and sigh when he brushes his fingers down my cheek.

"Let's just say I'm happy to have my wife back."

"They warned us when we started the whole fertility treatment thing that the hormones would make me wacky," I remind him.

"Well, they were right." He narrows his eyes at me. "I'm still pretty sure you were trying to kill me by hypothermia."

I giggle and kiss his chin. "The meds gave me hot flashes."

"Well, it's nice to have you back to normal, and I'm so damn thankful it worked."

God, I love him.

"Me too. The clinic called, checking in on me, and to let me know that in three months we can start trying again if we want to."

"So soon?" His eyes go wide and his hands still, while his body stiffens beneath me.

"Some couples start trying again right away because it can take so long for it to work, and we're not getting any younger."

"Not yet." He shakes his head adamantly and palms my cheek in his hand.

I frown up at him. I'm not ready to try again either, especially with as rigorous as fertility treatments are, but this response surprises me.

"What's wrong?" I ask. "I thought you wanted more."

"I do, but not yet. Sophie is four months old. We're still getting used to being parents. Besides," he swallows and kisses my forehead. "The emotional shit that came along with it not working for three years before we conceived Sophie was hard enough on me, but I know it was ten times harder on you. I'm just not ready to watch you go through that again. Not yet."

His magnificent blue eyes are fiercely serious, the frown-line between his them prominent. I reach up and smooth it with my middle finger.

"I'm not ready, either, Eyes. I'm happy with it being the three of us for a while."

"Good." He sighs and rests his forehead on mine. "Let's just enjoy our family for a while. Make love when we feel like it, rather than when a chart says we should."

I grin up at him. Having a normal sex life again sounds great to me.

"You know," I sit up, straddle his hips and run my fingers through his soft, dark blonde hair. One of his big hands cups my ass and the other trails leisurely up and down my spine.

"Yes?" he asks gruffly.

"There's nothing that says we can't practice." I grin down at him and nuzzle his nose.

He nods thoughtfully, as though he's considering my words carefully.

"True. Plus, there's this new technique I've wanted to try with you."

"Oh? And what is that?" My body begins to hum as he slides those hands under my shirt and over my skin, up my back, around to cup my breasts.

"Dirty Fireplace At A Lake Cabin Sex." He gives me that seductive smile and I giggle down at him.

"Oh, please, by all means, give me a demonstration."

"You don't have to ask me twice, baby."

Chapter Five

Thunk

I wake slowly, disoriented as I push my hair out of my face and look about the spacious bedroom. Shit! Sophie hasn't woken me up this morning! Then it dawns on me that I'm not in my own bedroom.

That's right, we're at the cabin. I smile as last night's events of making love by the fire flash through my mind. I glance over and frown at the empty bed.

My phone vibrates on the table next to me. It's a text from Gail; a photo of Sophie curled in her grandpa's arms, drinking her bottle and looking up at him while he reads the morning newspaper. *We're all fine. Don't worry. Enjoy yourselves.*

I smile and respond. *Thank you. We are. Love you guys. Will text later.*

I drop the phone to the bed and scrub my hands over my face and then hear it again.

Thunk

What the…?

I cross to the sliding door that leads out to the deck and pull the sheer curtains aside and gasp.

Snow! It freaking snowed! There must be six inches of soft white powder covering everything. It's absolutely breathtaking.

It never snows in Seattle, my ass.

Of course, we are up in the mountains, so Seattle might very well just be wet today.

Thunk.

What the hell is that?

I pull on my jeans and sweater, socks and shoes, and search the house. Isaac is nowhere to be found. I peek out the back door and find him near the lean-to by the house, splitting firewood.

Holy shit!

His faded blue jeans mold around his perfect ass and long legs. He's wearing a black t-shirt, and his fleece Northface jacket is lying over the railing nearby. The hair at the nape of his neck is dark with sweat.

He props another log on the stump, raises the axe over his head and brings it down with a loud *thunk*, sending the two new pieces flying in either direction.

God, the man is strong, and can do amazing things with tools.

I stand and just watch him for a moment, enjoying the view. The muscles in his shoulders flex and move with each swing of the axe.

I take a deep breath enjoying the scent of the pine trees and cold snow. It's not unbearably cold, just enough to make my cheeks pink and I can see my breath with each exhale. The snow has hushed everything around us, and it feels like we're the only two people for miles and miles.

Thunk.

Okay, time to get his attention. I grin slyly and gather a large hand full of snow, forming a ball, and take aim. I hit Isaac right at the back of his neck, sending cold snow down his shirt.

"What the hell?" He spins and glares at me. "Did you just throw snow at me?"

"Me?" I widen my eyes innocently. "I don't know what you're talking about."

"Uh, huh." He sets the axe down, removes his gloves and eyes me speculatively. "I'm not buying the innocent act."

I can't keep a straight face and I start to back up as he slowly advances.

"Really," a giggle escapes me. "I didn't do it."

"There's no one else here, baby."

"Maybe it fell out of a tree?" I ask hopefully and continue backing up. He bends down and gathers a large ball of snow in his hands, grins, and throws it at me, hitting me in the shoulder.

"Hey!" We stand, panting, grinning, and then sprint into action, gathering snow and throwing it at each other. He hits me way more than I hit him because I can't stop laughing long enough to really see where I'm throwing the damn snow.

"You're not good at this," he laughs.

"Shut up!" I throw another wad of snow, this time hitting him in the face. He shakes his head and brushes it off and glares at me.

"Now you've done it."

"I'm not scared of you," I taunt him and throw another handful of snow that lands nowhere near him.

"Nice try." He grins widely, his blue eyes on fire and suddenly runs toward me.

"Shit!" I squeal, my heart in my throat, and run away from him. I'm so about to get it.

He catches me easily, wraps an arm around my waist and tackles me to the ground, cushioning me against the hard ground with his own body, then rolling us so he's on top of me, pressing me into the soft, wet snow.

"You're in so much trouble," he murmurs.

"I swear," I giggle and twist beneath him, trying to get away. "I didn't do it."

"You are such a bad liar. You just threw about thirty snowballs at me."

"I didn't throw the first one."

"Uh, huh." He laughs and grabs a handful of snow and holds it over my face.

"Don't you dare!"

His eyes are dancing menacingly. "What'll you give me if I spare you?"

"A hug."

"Lame." Snow is smeared into my hair.

"Damn it!" I giggle and twist some more, but it's no use against his strong body.

"Try again."

Because it's my only defense, I grip his face in my hands and pull him down to me, kissing him thoroughly. His fingers burrow into my hair and he responds immediately, brushing his lips over mine, back and forth, then diving in deeply, his tongue dancing with mine.

I spread my legs, and he settles his hips between them, allowing me to cradle him, and I feel his erection against me.

"Mmm," I moan and roll my hips, making him gasp.

He slows the kiss, so it's lazy and unhurried, gently nibbling my lips.

"You're so sweet." He murmurs. "Look at me."

I open my eyes to see him gazing down at me, his hands are rhythmically brushing my hair.

"I love you, Stace."

"I love you too, Eyes."

He smiles lovingly, kisses my lips chastely, then my forehead and pushes himself off me, pulling me with him.

"Come on," he keeps my hand in his and pulls me toward the house, trudging through the slippery snow.

"Where are we going?" I ask breathlessly.

"Shower. I'm sweaty and I want you naked."

Yes, please.

He's in a hurry. He leads me through the house, heedlessly leaving a trail of wet snow behind us, to the master suite. "Strip," he commands and leaves me to start the shower in the impressive bathroom.

I grin as I hear the water start. I love it when he gets all bossy and sexy on me. I quickly peel my wet clothes off and pile them at the end of the bed. I'll wash them later. Isaac stalks out of the bathroom, all naked, his face still determined, and… *all mine.*

Instead of leading me back into the bathroom, he sweeps me up into his arms, startling me.

"Whoa! Someone's impatient."

He grins down at me and kisses me hard and fast.

"I've been waiting all morning for you to wake up. You were so tired, I wanted to let you sleep in, but I've been desperate to be inside you. So I decided to split the wood to relieve some of the energy."

"You don't seem to be lacking in energy," I reply dryly.

"Yeah, it didn't work."

He carries me into the shower and gently sets me on my feet. This shower is freaking huge. The tile is dark brown and gold, and there are multiple shower heads at different heights, as well as a rain head directly over us. The water is hot and quickly fogging up the entire bathroom.

Isaac pushes me into the hot water and grabs my shower gel. He squirts it into his palm and rubs his hands together, creating lather. He closes his eyes and breathes in deeply.

"I love the smell of this. I love smelling it on you all day." His hands glide over my torso, my breasts and arms. My head falls back on a sigh as I enjoy the gentle strokes of his expert hands.

"Turn around," he murmurs and I comply. He lathers my back in broad strokes, massaging and kneading my muscles. "You are so fucking sexy, baby."

I moan in response and lean back against his chest, lay my head on his shoulder. He wraps his arms around me as the water cascades down our bodies, rinsing the soap from my body.

"My turn," I murmur and turn in his arms to face him. I mirror his movements from earlier with his body wash, lather my hands, and glide them over his wet, muscular body. He closes his eyes and sighs, enjoying my touch.

I wash every sexy, hard inch of him, trace the tattoo on his shoulder blade with my fingertip, rinse him thoroughly, and then drop to my knees.

"Fuck," he whispers.

I grin and grip the base of his hard cock and tease the tip with my tongue, brushing it over the slit. He sucks in a deep breath through his teeth and twists his fingers in my hair and I slowly sink over him, taking him as far as I can into my mouth. I sheathe my teeth in my lips and pull up, sucking hard, and roll my tongue around the tip.

Before I can sink down again, he grips my shoulders and pulls me to my feet.

"Hey, I wasn't…"

"Enough. You'll make me come, and I need to be inside you." He grips my ass in both hands and lifts me. "Wrap your legs around me."

He pushes me against the tile wall and buries himself inside me as I wrap my legs around him.

"Oh, God." I push my hands into his hair and hold on for dear life as he slams into me over and over, like a man possessed. His face is buried in my neck, his breathing ragged and feral.

"You feel so good." He shakes his head. "So fucking good."

I can't make myself respond. One of his hands slides from my ass up to my breast. He pinches and pulls on the nipple, making me cry out.

"Can't get enough of you," he whispers. He's pinned me completely to the wall with his body. My hips are pulsing and rolling with him, meeting his thrusts.

"God, Eyes," I murmur. He lifts his head and looks up at me with raging blue eyes as he speeds up, grinding harder against my core. "Oh, babe, I'm gonna…"

"Fuck yes, come baby."

My legs tighten around him and I let go, fire bursting through me. Isaac thrusts once more, rocks himself against me, hard, and then buries his face in my neck again, groaning loudly as he spills himself inside me.

He holds me there for a few moments as our breathing calms. He kisses my neck, then my jaw, and finally my lips, softly and lovingly.

"I'm not done," he whispers. My eyes open wide and I stare at him.

"You're not?"

"No." He runs his fingers down my cheek and sighs. Before I can ask him what he's thinking, he says, "But I'm hungry, and we're going to need our strength."

Chapter Six

"Oh, look!" I turn my phone toward Isaac. "Your mom just sent me a photo of Sophie napping with your dad."

"How many photos does that make now?" He asks with a chuckle and aims the remote toward the tv.

"I don't know, about fifty." I smirk and respond to Gail. "It makes me feel better knowing that she's okay. I'm really missing her."

"I know, me too. But are you having fun?"

"I am. Thank you." I smile over at him as he pulls my feet up in his lap. I finish the sandwich Isaac fixed us for lunch and fire up my Kindle. "Do you care if I read for a while?"

"Do you care if I watch a Statham movie?"

"Nope." I settle back with my book and sigh as Isaac begins to run his thumb up and down the arch of my foot. "You're so good at that."

"Lots of practice on my pregnant wife," he smiles warmly at me.

"You took very good care of me when I was pregnant."

"It's my job to take care of you, baby." He continues to rub my feet while Jason Statham drives a car through Paris, and I'm completely content in this moment. I wish Sophie was here, curled up with us, but I know she's safe and loved, and I'm enjoying my husband.

"Do you want something to drink?" he asks.

"Sure, some tea would be great."

"I'll get it." He unfolds himself from the couch and walks into the kitchen to set on a pot of water.

"I could get used to all this spoiling, you know." I call out to him.

"You deserve it. I know that you work hard at home, for me and Soph. You deserve to be pampered once in a while."

And just like that, I fall in love with him all over again.

"Have you been talking to Luke?" I ask.

"Uh, no, why?"

"Because he's the over-the-top romantic in this family."

"Trust me, this is not over-the-top romantic."

"To a woman who has barely had time to take a shower for the past four months, this is incredibly romantic."

"Stace, do you want to hire some help? Maybe just a few days a week?"

I wave him off and shake my head. "No, I don't need help. You know I love nothing more than being a mom and taking care of our girl. I'm lucky to be able to stay home with her and take care of you guys. I'm just saying thank you. This is very sweet and I love you."

He pins me with heated blue eyes as he fills my mug full of hot water. "I love you too."

He settles in next to me again, pulls my feet back into his lap and I sip my tea and enjoy my book while he gets lost in his movie.

***

"I can't believe you let me sleep so long this afternoon." I smile at my sexy husband and sip the wine he poured me for dinner. We are curled up again in front of the fireplace, enjoying the quiet and our last evening alone together.

"You needed it. Besides, it could be a while before you get another nap." He grins and then unfolds himself from the couch and leans down to kiss my forehead. "I'll be right back."

"Okay."

I sit back against the soft cushions of the couch and smile. These past few days have been the best. Isaac's always been good to me. He's an affectionate and attentive husband. But, as in most relationships, we've grown comfortable and I admit that it's easy to take each other for granted. I wouldn't say that romance is dead, but there are times she goes on vacation.

Especially when we were dealing with infertility issues and having sex for the sake of knocking me up. It makes me feel so good that he is making such an effort to be romantic. We needed to reconnect.

"Hey, don't you dare go back to sleep on me, babe." I didn't even realize I'd closed my eyes. I smile up at him and take a deep breath. I love this black t-shirt on him, the way it clings to his abs and sits on his hips.

"You look good," I murmur. His eyes heat and one side of his mouth tips up into a lazy smile.

"You're not so bad yourself. C'mon." He takes my hand and pulls me up off the couch. "You don't need any more of this if it's just going to make you sleep." He takes my wine from me and sets it on the kitchen island as we walk past it and up the stairs.

"We're going to bed already?"

"Nope." He smiles down at me, and when we reach the top of the stairs, instead of heading to the master suite, he pulls me in the other direction, toward a spare bedroom. I gasp as we walk inside.

The covers on the double sized bed have been pulled all the way off, leaving the soft blue fitted sheet covering the mattress, and the matching top sheet pulled back. There are at least a dozen candles lit all over the room, sending shadows over the space. Soft music is playing through a small sound system in the corner.

Isaac pulls me against him, his front to my back and wraps his arms around me, kissing my hair, then turns me around and pulls my shirt up over my head, letting it fall to the floor.

"I think you need a massage," he murmurs and slips my bra off, throwing it on top of my shirt.

"You do?" I ask dryly.

"Yes," he responds simply. He pulls my jeans and panties off, bending down to slip them over my feet. He stands and kisses my lips gently, cupping my face in his hands. "Lie on the bed, on your stomach," he whispers.

"Okay." Like I'm gonna say no to that.

I lie on my stomach and let out a big sigh.

"No sleeping," Isaac says with a chuckle.

"I don't know what's wrong with me. I'm never this tired," I respond with a smile.

"You're relaxed. I'm glad, honey. That was the point of taking a few days away." I hear him rub his hands together and then they're on my back, firmly stroking in a long line down the sides of my spine, over my bare ass, around my hips and up my sides to my shoulder blades, and then he does it again, making long, broad strokes over my back.

"Oh God, I love you." I moan.

He laughs and starts to massage my low back in slow, firm circles. "Feel good?" he murmurs with a smile in his voice.

"Mmmm."

He works his way up and down my back, then over my butt again and down each leg, gently yet firmly working my muscles into submission.

"You're so good with your hands, Eyes. This is why I married you."

"Is this the only reason?" he asks.

"This and your ass."

His hands stop moving.

"My ass?" he asks, his voice amused.

"Your ass. You have a great ass."

"I don't think you've ever told me that."

"I didn't want to over-inflate your ego."

He smacks my ass, sending a loud slap through the room. I push up to my elbows with a gasp.

"Hey!"

"I like your ass too. It's slapable."

"Slapable? I don't think that's a word." I lay back down to enjoy his roaming hands.

"I don't care. It is."

"It grew even more slapable with Sophie." I murmur and grin.

"Your ass did not grow," he mutters.

"Do you need glasses?"

"It didn't."

"Whatever. I think there are still stretch marks back there to prove you wrong."

"Shut up."

"Does it bother you?" I ask and push up to my elbows again, looking back at him. He's frowning, the lines between his eyebrows prominent.

"Does what bother me?"

"The change in my body. The stretch marks, the pouch on my belly that might never go away."

His hands stop and he looks me in the eye, his gaze worried. "Do they bother you?"

"Not really. We worked hard for these changes." I shrug and look down.

"Look at me." His hard voice surprises me. "I don't see the changes, Stace. I see my wife." He shrugs, and I don't know why but that simple statement makes me want to cry. "I've been hot after you since the first moment I saw you in that bar in college."

I just stare at him. Well, shit he's sweet.

His hands resume their course over my skin and I sigh and lay my head back on the bed.

"I'll tell you what I do see," he murmurs and runs his thumb up the middle of my right calf. "Soft, smooth skin." His touch lightens, and now it's just his fingertips, moving up and down my legs, tickling that sensitive spot behind my knees, and traveling up and over my bottom to my back.

"Firm ass, dimples at the small of your back that are sexy as fuck." He leans down and kisses my dimples, runs his tongue over them and then chastely kisses them again.

"Strong shoulders," he murmurs, brushing his fingers over them and up into my hair. "The most beautiful hair I've ever had my hands in. It's thick and heavy, and the color... right now with the candlelight, it looks like it's on fire."

Fuck me.

"Turn over," he whispers in my ear. I comply and look up into his molten blue eyes. He pushes my hair off my face and offers me a gentle smile. "I see flecks of gold in your eyes, and when you're turned on like you are right now, they shine. And your lips…" He kisses me softly and runs his thumb over my lower lip. "Your lips are soft and pink and say the sweetest things."

He slowly makes his way down my chin and neck, kissing and nibbling. My body is moving beneath him, writhing. I'm completely seduced by him; my body by his touch and my mind and heart with his words.

"Your breasts are perfect." He gently suckles one nipple, then the other and makes his way down to my belly, tickling me with his nose and lips.

He gently traces the evidence of my pregnancy with his fingertip. "These aren't ugly, baby." He nuzzles my belly. "We did work hard for them, and you earned them. They're fading. But even if they never go away, every mark was worth it. Because without them, we wouldn't have Soph." He looks up at me and I run my fingers through his hair. I have tears in my eyes.

"When did you get so good with words?" I whisper.

He shakes his head and kisses my belly again. "I know I don't tell you enough how sexy you are. But don't ever doubt that I love your body, just the way it is, no matter how it changes."

His fingers glide down my stomach, over my pubis and to my folds. Isaac grins.

"This is another of my favorite places."

"Is that right?" I grin back at him and sigh as he sinks one finger inside me while his thumb dances around my clit.

"Oh, definitely." He scoots further down the bed and opens my core, his thumbs parting my lips. "Look how beautiful you are. Pink and wet." His lips glide from my clit down through my labia, then he uses his tongue to trace back up again. "Delicious," he whispers.

Chapter Seven

My back arches off the bed as his tongue plunges into my core. "Oh my God."

"So responsive." He adds a second finger and swirls that magical tongue around my nub, teasing and flicking it, then sucking it gently.

"Fuck, Eyes…"

"Oh, yes, we will, but I'm having fun down here for now, sweetheart." He smiles mischievously and kisses that spot he knows, the place where my thigh meets my center, and I moan again, gripping the sheet tightly in my fingers.

He pulls both fingers out of me, pushing them through my lips, around my clit, making me even wetter, his intensely blue eyes watching his fingers play with me.

"So beautiful," he whispers to himself and then looks up at me, grins widely and shedding his clothes quickly, climbs over me. He rests his pelvis between my legs, and settles down on me, just looking at me.

"What's wrong?" I ask.

"Absolutely nothing." He kisses me chastely, gently sweeping his lips across mine. He rocks his hips, sliding himself through my wetness, and then slowly, oh so very slowly, inches into me until he's filled me completely and he's buried inside me.

I wrap my arms around his shoulders and my legs around his hips, holding him close and he rests his forehead against mine.

"The best thing I ever did in my life was make you mine, Stace," he whispers. I grasp his face in my hands and nuzzle his nose, letting tears fall down my face. He brushes them gently with his thumbs and ever so slowly, starts to move his hips. He pulls one leg up over his shoulder and turns his head to kiss my calf. I gasp at the new angle, allowing him to slide into me even deeper. And suddenly, I can't stand slow and steady any more. I need it fast and I need it hard.

I move my hips, pumping them up and down, squeezing around him.

"God, babe, don't squeeze me so hard. You'll make me come."

"That's the point."

He shakes his head adamantly. "I don't want to come yet."

I grip his ass in my hands and pull him harder and clasp around him tighter. He scowls down at me and pulls all the way out.

"Hey!"

"You're not good at doing what you're told, are you?"

"Ten years of marriage and you're just now figuring this out?" I ask dryly.

He slams into me again, hard, and then pulls all the way out.

"Argh!" Damn him!

Now he teases me, putting just the tip inside, grinning proudly at me. "Ready to do what you're told?"

I raise my hips quickly, making his cock slide farther into me, but he pulls out.

"Oh no. I think you'd better turn over."

Effortlessly, he flips me over, pulls my ass in the air and buries himself inside me, his hands gripping my hips, pulling me on and off of him at a punishing, yet steady pace.

"Oh, God." He covers me with his chest and reaches around to circle my clit with his fingers.

"I make you come, baby, then you can make me come. That's how it works." His raspy voice, and those magical fingers, and the incessant push and pull of friction inside me sends me over the edge and I cry out his name as I come, pulsating and shuddering beneath him helplessly.

"That's it, beautiful. Oh, God, Stace…"

And suddenly he's brutally gripping my hips again and pushing inside me, as hard and as deep as he can, and I feel him spill his seed inside me.

"Fuck me," he whispers and kisses my shoulder.

"I just did."

"Smart ass."

***

"What's wrong?" Isaac cups my face in his hands with a frown and looks down at me as our family walks ahead of us, not paying any attention to us.

"Just a small headache." I smile reassuringly, take his hand in mine and kiss it, then he tucks them both in his jacket pocket to keep them warm.

We're walking around Woodland Park Zoo in the heart of Seattle enjoying the Christmas light display they put on every year. It's early evening and the air is crisp, making our cheeks pink and noses cold. We've had a rare winter dry-spell the last few days. Actually, since we returned from the cabin a few weeks ago the weather has been surprisingly mild. Perfect Zoo Light weather.

The zoo strings hundreds of thousands of lights, all throughout the zoo, in shapes of animals and flowers and landscape scenes. It's really quite beautiful after dark. They also bring in reindeer and a huge carousel for the kids.

This is an annual family outing for the Montgomerys. This year it's just Isaac's parents, Isaac, Soph and I, Jules, and Nat and Luke. Brynna came along as well with her two adorable five-year-old twin girls, Maddie and Josie.

"You've had a few headaches over the past couple weeks," Isaac comments. He pat's Sophie's back as she squirms in her sleep in the sling across his chest.

"I'm okay." I smile at him again and then laugh as the girls squeal in delight when they see a fairytale light display, hopping up and down, wanting to get a better look. Brynna looks back at us, surveys the area quickly and turns back to the girls.

"God, I'm gonna throw up." Jules mutters. Luke and Nat are kissing. *Again.* I laugh and rub Jules' arm in comfort.

"Aren't you used to them making out by now?"

"Jesus, do they have to do it all the damn time?"

Luke grins, kisses Nat one last time and wraps his arm around her. "Yes."

"Yuck." Jules sticks her tongue out and shudders and I can't help but laugh.

"Are you nine?" Isaac asks.

"Shut up, Isaac," Jules responds.

Suddenly, Isaac grips the lapels of my wool coat and gently pulls me up to his lips, kissing me hard and deep. I hear Jules gag, and I giggle, wrap my arms around his neck and give into his passionate embrace, mindful that Sophie is now snuggled between us.

"Good one, Isaac," Natalie remarks, impressed as we separate.

"Why should you guys get all the fun?" Isaac asks, still smiling down at me.

Why indeed?

"There are children here, you know," Jules reminds us.

"I want to feed the reindeer," Maddie jumps up and down and her sister joins her.

"Okay, reindeer it is," Isaac says and motions for everyone to walk further down the pathway. Brynna looks over her shoulder, toward the way we've just come and frowns.

"Brynna's been looking over her shoulder all evening," I whisper at Isaac. He glances over at her thoughtfully.

"Hey," Isaac drapes an arm around her and gives her a squeeze, then pulls away. "You're safe here."

She offers him a small smile. "I know. I just can't help but stay alert."

I take her hand in my free one as the three of us lag behind the rest. "Are you going to tell me what happened?"

Her face drops and she stares down at the ground. She bites her bottom lip and turns her dark brown eyes up to me and shakes her head, her dark curls bouncing around her pretty face. "No."

"Why?" I ask in frustration.

"It's just better for you if you don't know."

I look over at Isaac. "Do you know?"

He shakes his head and scowls over at Brynna. "No. She's a stubborn mule."

"Matt and I have it under control," she mutters.

"Right, so looking over your shoulder everywhere you go, getting a new disposable cell phone with a new number and changing your hair color are keeping it under control? What's next, Bryn, you gonna change your names and social security numbers too?"

She glares at me and I think I see tears start to form. I feel like a bitch.

"Shit, I'm sorry." I shake my head and exhale deeply. "That was horrible. I'm just worried about you, and you've never kept secrets from me before."

"I'm just trying to keep you safe."

"Okay." She looks up at me, surprised. "Okay. When you can tell me, come tell me."

"So, Brynna," Isaac starts. "I'm assuming you could use a job."

She cringes. "Yeah, but I don't really want to start applying and having prospective employers run a background check. It'll draw attention."

"Right.," Isaac nods. "Well, I need help in my office. I need someone to answer the phone, take care of billing, things like that."

"I thought you already had someone for that," she frowns.

"I do, but business is good, and we need more help. You in?"

"You're offering me a job?"

"Yep."

She bites her lip, considering his offer.

"Under the table, Bryn."

"Really?"

He just smiles over at her, and I just love him so much.

"I can start tomorrow." She smiles big, the first true smile I've seen on her beautiful face since she got home almost two weeks ago and launches herself at him, hugging him as closely as she can with Sophie strapped to his chest.

"Hey, watch your hands, sister," I mutter playfully. "And don't crush my baby."

She laughs.

"If he wasn't yours, I'd claim him."

"Ladies, no need to fight. There's enough of me to go around."

We both bust into giggles, and Isaac frowns. "Trust me babe, you've got your hands full with what you have."

"Killjoy."

"Mom! Mom! I'm gonna feed the 'deer!" Josie screams and runs up to her mother in excitement.

"Great, Jose! How many are there?"

"Eight."

"What are their names?" Luke asks her and winks at Brynna.

I can't help but laugh at Brynna's response to Luke. She blushes like a teenager whenever he looks at her. She still can't believe that Natalie is married to *the* Luke Williams.

"Donner, Dasher…" Josie starts.

"Blitzen and Cupid…" Maddie adds, and scrunches up her face, thinking hard.

"Comet and Vixen and Dancer and… and…" Josie and Maddie look at each other, counting on their little fingers.

"And Lucky!" Maddie cries!

"Lucky?" Luke asks with a surprised laugh. We all try to hide our snickers behind our hands, but fail miserably.

"Yep."

"Sounds good to me."

"Auntie Stace, Sophie wants to feed the deer," Josie says earnestly.

"I think Sophie is too little to feed the deer, sweetie," I smile down at her and pull her soft, long raven braid through my hand.

"Well, can I look at her then?" she asks and Isaac squats, letting the sweet little girl look in the sling at the sleeping baby. Both girls have been a bit obsessed with their little cousin since meeting her for the first time. "Oh, she's sleeping," she whispers loudly at Isaac.

"Yes, she is," he responds with a grin. I can't help but smile at them.

"Why?" she gazes earnestly into Isaac's eyes, which are eye-level with hers.

"Cause she's sleepy."

Josie smiles sweetly. "Okay."

And off she goes to continue feeding the deer with her sister.

"You're good with kids, Isaac," Jules says casually while watching her parents help the girls feed the animals.

"What do you want, brat?"

"I can't say something nice to you without wanting something?"

Isaac laughs and tucks Sophie's binkie in her mouth. "Okay, thanks. I think."

"For the love of the baby Jesus in a manger will you stop!" Jules suddenly exclaims and we all break out laughing at the sight of Natalie and Luke in another passionate embrace.

"Give it up, Jules." Luke mutters and dips Natalie low, giving us all a show.

"God, I hate you."

Chapter Eight

"We're sitting in the back," Isaac murmurs in my ear as we enter the movie theater. It's a weeknight, so there aren't many other movie-goers in the plush seats.

"I'm so not making out with you in a movie theater," I mumble and hear him chuckle.

"Yes you will."

"I'm not sixteen."

I climb the steps to the top and we claim seats directly in the middle. We are in a theater that offers reclining leather loveseats rather than the typical theater seats. It's new, and I swear to God, I'm never going to another run-of-the-mill theater ever again. Isaac raises the armrest, effectively converting the space into a cozy leather loveseat. We settle in and wait for the movie to start.

"I can't believe you agreed to watch a chick flick," I shove a handful of popcorn in my mouth and take a sip of soda.

"I don't plan on watching much of it."

"I'm *not* making out with you during the movie. I've been waiting for this movie to come out for weeks."

"I'll buy it for you on Blu Ray." He shrugs and bites his hotdog almost in half.

"Then why did we spend almost fifty dollars to come to the movies?" I ask.

He grins at me and swallows. "Movie Makeout Date."

"Excuse me?" I ask with a laugh.

"We're on a date."

"Clearly."

"At the movies."

"Okay." I frown up at him and then immediately return his lazy smile. God I love it when he looks at me like that. His eyes are all happy and cocky.

"Where it's dark." He pulls me closer to his side and wraps his arm around me, resting his hand on my hip and whispers in my ear, "and no one can see me touch you."

Holy shit, he just turned me on in a movie theater.

"How long have you had this little daydream?" I ask him dryly.

"Since I was about thirteen."

I laugh and rest my head on his shoulder while I munch on my popcorn. A few more patrons file in and find seats, well below our perch in the back row.

The lights dim as the movie starts. After fifteen minutes, I set my popcorn tub on the floor, having had my fill, and lean back into my warm husband. He shifts in the wide seat until his back is against the armrest and he pulls me between his legs, wraps his arms protectively around my shoulders, and kisses my hair.

With a big sigh, I relax into him. The actors in the movie are passionately arguing, and then are suddenly kissing, just as passionately. Isaac's hand roams from my shoulder blade down to my ass, where he gently rubs small circles around my derriere.

He's not going to give up on his quest to make out.

He tips my chin up and brushes his lips across mine, so lightly I can barely feel it. It's just a whisper of a kiss. His lips tickle the sides of my mouth, my jaw line. He gently kisses my nose. His hand sinks into my hair and he claims my mouth again, still with absolute gentleness.

I sigh against him, and open my lips for him, inviting him to take the kiss deeper, and he answers my invitation eagerly, dipping his tongue inside to play and tease mine, then nibbling my lips again. He pulls back and brushes my hair rhythmically with his fingers.

"Watch the movie," he whispers.

Oh right, the movie.

I lay my head back on his chest and feel him kiss my hair and grin. The hand on my ass pulls up and then slides back down, under my jeans, and cups my cheek firmly. His large, warm hand feels heavenly, and I have to physically put my hand over my mouth to keep from moaning out loud.

He's such a tease!

His other hand moves down from my hair, over my shoulder, and he brushes the backs of his fingers against the side of my breast, then back up again to my neck, where he *knows* I'm the most sensitive and very gently moves his thumb back and forth over the spot that makes me tingle all over.

Okay, we can both play this game.

I run my hand firmly down his side, against his ribs, to his hip and under his t-shirt so I can feel his abs. God, they're so toned and hard. And warm. And clenching and flinching under my touch.

I grin and continue to tickle him lightly, with just my fingertips, tracing the ridges of his muscles up around his ribs. His erection is growing against my stomach but my eyes are still glued to the screen, although I have absolutely no idea what's happening in the movie at this point, I shift to the side and unbutton his jeans and slip my hand inside.

He gasps softly as I grip his hardness in my palm and tease him. The hand on my ass clenches and moves down between my slick folds. "Wet," he murmurs against my hair and he kisses my head.

Suddenly he pushes me back, buttons his jeans and yanks me out of the seat, pulling me behind him to the isle and down the steps.

"Where are we going?" I whisper loudly.

He doesn't answer until we're out of the theater and walking down the sidewalk.

"Eyes, what are you doing? The movie…" He pushes me up against the wall and pins me with his body, holds my wrists up at the side of my head and he kisses me voraciously, consuming me and making love to me with his mouth.

"Blu Ray," he growls, his eyes molten blue and he's pulling me behind him again to the car. "I need to get you home and naked. Now."

"Well, okay then."

***

Where did all these packages come from? I'd just poured myself my first cup of coffee and was headed back upstairs to shower and get ready for the day before Sophie wakes up, but when I pass by the Christmas tree, there are at least a dozen brightly wrapped gifts with big bows added to the gifts I'd already wrapped and placed under the tree last week.

Setting my coffee on an end table, I kneel on the floor and reach for a big red box with a gold bow.

"Hands off."

I snatch my hand back and sit on my heels and look back at Isaac guiltily. "I didn't touch anything."

"You were about to."

"Where did these come from?" I ask and gaze back at the pretty boxes.

"Uh, Santa?" I glare back at him.

"It's not Christmas morning, smart ass."

"Calling Santa a smart ass is not being a nice girl. Keep being naughty, and you'll get coal."

"I'll show you naughty…"

Sophie's whimpers come through the baby monitor, and I know I only have twenty minutes, tops, to shower before she'll insist that it's time to get out of her crib for the day.

"I'll take a rain check," Isaac murmurs and pulls me against him as I climb to my feet. "Later tonight?" he asks just before his lips brush over mine.

"It's a date." I grin and kiss his lightly stubbled chin, enjoying the way it feels against my lips.

"What are you up to today?" he asks.

"I'm taking Sophie to my mom's this morning. She asked if she could keep her for a few hours, so I thought I'd take advantage of it and go to the grocery store and maybe get a pedicure. Your coffee's on the kitchen counter."

"Thanks, baby. Enjoy your quiet time." He grins and kisses me on his way out the door to work.

"Don't work too hard."

***

"But, I don't understand," I reply to nurse Kimberly. "Why do I need to come back in? I was just in yesterday."

"The blood work we ran yesterday has come back from the lab, Stacy, and the doctor would like to go over some things."

What things?

"He said that everything was okay, and you'd be calling to let me know that the labs were normal. You can just give me the results now."

I'm on my way from the grocery store to the nail salon to get that pedicure I so desperately need. Another unnecessary trip to the doctor seems ridiculous and a waste of time.

"I'm not at liberty to discuss the results of the tests over the phone. Dr. Wilson needs to see you. He has an opening in an hour. Can we expect you then?"

Well, hell, there goes the pedicure.

"Yeah, I'll be there." I hang up the phone with a scowl. More doctor appointments. Isaac talked me into going yesterday because I've still been having headaches. They're not debilitating, but they are frequent. The doctor suspected that they were due to stress, but ran labs just to make sure everything was on track.

Everything had better be on track and this is just routine or I'm gonna punch somebody in the throat. I'm done with doctors for a while.

My phone rings again, and I smile when I see it's Brynna.

"Hey."

"Hey, I'm leaving your mom's. She has Sophie and offered to keep the girls for me too. Where are you?"

"I was going to get a pedicure…" before I can finish the sentence, Brynna gasps.

"Without me? What the fuck?"

"It's a good thing the girls aren't with you," I reply dryly.

"I know. I try to get all the swear words out when they're not around."

"As I was saying, I was going to get a pedi, but my doctor just called and they want me to go in for a follow up instead."

"You're still having follow-up visits at almost five months post-partum?" she asks.

"No, I went in because I've been having headaches. I guess there's some blood work they want to talk about."

"Oh. Well, since I don't have the girls, want company? We can do lunch after."

"Sure, thanks. I'll meet you there." I rattle off the address to her and end the call. I pull into the office parking lot and wait for Brynna in my car. It doesn't take her long to join me.

"Hi, Fran," I greet the receptionist. "Dr. Wilson wanted to see me again today."

"He's expecting you. Thanks for coming on such short notice. No Sophie today?" she asks with a smile.

"No, I had a babysitter today."

Nurse Kimberly comes around the corner and smiles at me. "Oh great, you're here. I'll take you back."

"It's not terribly busy today." I'm trying to make small talk to calm my nerves. I hate the doctor office. You'd think with all the dozens, if not hundreds, of hours I've spent in them over the past three years it wouldn't bother me.

It does.

"This time of year is usually slow. Especially this week, the week of Christmas." Kimberly offers a friendly smile at Brynna.

"Oh, I'm sorry. This is my cousin, Brynna."

"Nice to meet you. Okay, have a seat, the doctor will be right with you."

"This place gives me the heebs," Brynna remarks after the nurse leaves. She shivers and looks at a plastic vagina. "What the fuck do they put these things out here for, anyway? I don't want to see a plastic model of the jay-jay."

"It's to scare us into not having sex anymore."

"It's working."

There's a brief knock on the door, startling Brynna and then the door swings open, and my handsome doctor, Dr. Delicious Wilson briskly walks in the room.

"Thanks for coming in, Stacy."

"Sure. This is my cousin Brynna."

"Brynna." He automatically shakes her hand, not looking up from the chart in his hand. Bryn catches my eye, her own big brown eyes wide and mouths, *Holy shit!*

I know! I respond.

"So, Stacy, I know we discussed yesterday that the headaches are most likely due to stress, and not related to the minor gestational diabetes that you had in the latter part of your pregnancy."

"Right," I nod.

"And that may still very well be the case because your labs are perfectly normal in regards to your blood sugars."

"Good." I smile and drape my handbag over my shoulder, expecting to leave with the results of my test.

"However," he continues and I halt my movements. "You're pregnant."

"The fuck?" Brynna mutters and then breaks out into hysterical giggles.

Chapter Nine

I stare at Delicious for a few seconds, my mouth gaping, my eyes wide, and then Brynna's giggles break through the fog surrounding my brain.

"I'm sorry, what did you say?"

"You're pregnant."

And just like that, just as the giggles were under control, Brynna lets loose again.

"Has she been drinking?" the doctor asks.

"No. This is just crazy. You might want to double check those lab results, doc. I'm not pregnant."

"Uh, yeah, you are."

I'm stunned. I blink at him.

"Only you, Stacy." Brynna takes a deep breath and wipes a tear from her eye. "Only you would struggle through infertility treatments for three years, finally have a baby, and then get pregnant again right away without even trying."

"I've seen it before," Doc responds. "Sometimes a woman's system sort of 'resets' itself after a pregnancy, and she's able to get pregnant right way."

Huh.

"When was your last menstrual cycle?" he asks.

"I don't remember. Probably before I got pregnant with Sophie. I just thought my hormones hadn't leveled out from the pregnancy yet."

"So you probably got pregnant a couple months ago."

"Tahiti?" Brynna mutters.

Tahiti.

"Shit, I've had alcohol! I wasn't breast feeding Soph, so I've had drinks here and there since Tahiti."

"More than a few on a daily basis?" he asks.

"No, more like a few a month."

"You're fine," he smiles reassuringly. "You know the drill. Call your OB and set up an ultrasound and consult."

"So, everything else is okay?" I ask.

"Yep, you're great. Best of luck to you."

I stare at Brynna for a minute, my mouth opening and shutting like a fish out of water.

"Lunch," she says and takes my hand, pulling me out of the office. What is it with everyone pulling me all over the place lately?

"I have to take my groceries home and get Sophie."

"We'll take your groceries home, put away the perishables, and then go to lunch. Your mom is enjoying Sophie."

"Okay."

"Can you drive?"

"Yeah, why?"

"Because you're trying to unlock your car with your lip gloss rather than your key fob."

I look down at the lip gloss in my hand. "Shit."

"I'll drive, we'll leave my car here, and I'll have my dad come get it later."

"Okay."

"How do you feel?" she asks as we pull in the driveway. I'm still staring numbly ahead in shock.

"Not pregnant."

"Come on, let's do this so we can go."

We quickly unload the bags of groceries from the car to the kitchen and stow all the food that belongs in the freezer or fridge away, and before I know it, we're back in the car and pulling into a nearby Mexican restaurant.

"We're getting margaritas." She grins over at me. "We'll make yours a virgin."

"Fuck, no alcohol for another year."

We're seated and I greedily dig into the warm basket of tortilla chips and salsa.

"Nothing wrong with your appetite," Brynna states dryly.

"Shut up." I eat two more chips and take a sip of my virgin margarita. "This is no margarita."

"So…" Brynna lifts an eyebrow expectantly.

"So what?"

"Don't be stubborn. Talk." She takes a bite of a chip and a long sip of her slutty margarita and smiles smugly.

"I hate you right now."

"No you don't." She waves me off with a flick of the wrist. "How do you feel about the baby?"

"Oh, Sophie's great. She's so funny, she just giggles all the time. Here, I've got a video on my phone I want to show you…" I look up into Brynna's wide brown eyes. "What?"

"Stace, are you having a seizure? Do I have to take you back to Dr. Delectable?"

"He's Dr. Delicious."

"Whatever, I'll take you back to Dr. Sex-on-a-stick if I need to. You do remember that tid-bit about you being preggers, right?"

"Oh." I sit back in the seat, a chip hanging limply between my fingers. "Yeah."

"Right."

"I'm pregnant." I say the words again in my brain, letting them sit there and percolate. "Without meds, or shots in the hip, or being told, month after month, that it didn't work."

Holy shit.

"What do you think Isaac will say?" she asks.

I flinch. "Well, coincidentally, we talked about this a few weeks ago. We were gonna wait to have more, but I'm quite sure he'll be happy once the shock wears off." I shrug. Yes, Isaac will be great. We'd planned to have a whole houseful of children when we first got married.

"Oh, God." I swallow another chip and take a sip of water.

"What?" Brynna asks.

"I'm going to have two babies under eighteen months old. Two babies in diapers. Two babies…"

Her eyebrows are raised and she's grinning. "I wouldn't know what that's like at all."

"Damn, I was not expecting this." I laugh and take a deep breath. "Sophie's gonna be a big sister."

"How are you going to tell him?"

"Oh, I don't know. It should be something fun." I clap my hands excitedly.

"I know! Christmas is just a few days away."

"I like where you're going with this." I sip my margarita impostor and lean forward, listening intently.

"Okay, I saw this on that pinning board online. Have you seen that site?"

"I'm addicted to that site." I waste many, many hours on that site.

"Here's what you're going to do: call Natalie first. Then…"

***

"How was your day?" Isaac asks and pulls me in for a kiss. He's just come in from work, and brought Italian with him, God love him.

"It was a good day," I smile to myself and jump up and down in my head. "Pretty standard."

"Anything new happen?"

You have no fucking idea, babe.

"Not really." I shrug and kiss him chastely and then start pulling Styrofoam boxes of delicious food out of a brown paper bag. Isaac walks into the kitchen for plates and silverware and pulls down two wine goblets and a bottle of Merlot.

Shit.

"No wine for me, Eyes," I say as nonchalantly as possible.

"You sure? I know you love this with the chicken parmesan." He frowns and tilts his head. "Are you feeling okay?"

"I'm fine," I wave him off and dish up our plates, smiling over at Sophie who is sitting in her bouncy seat on the table, blowing raspberries and playing with her feet.

"No more headaches?" he asks and returns the wine and goblets to the kitchen, bringing us each a bottle of water instead.

"No, not in a couple days." I grin at him. "Definitely no head-ache tonight." I wiggle my eyebrows, making him chuckle and doing my best to distract him from talking too much about my day.

"Did the doctor call with the results of yesterday's tests?" he asks and takes a bite of salad.

So much for that.

"Yeah, everything's fine." I can't look him in the eye now. I hate lying to him, even if it's to surprise him. And this is a *big* deal, and I'm so excited! Maybe I should tell him...

"So, the headaches were probably from stress then?" he asks, looking thoughtful while he chews.

"That's what the doctor thinks." I take a sip of water and dig back into my saucy pasta. God, it's good.

"I know you've had a lot on your plate, Stace. Maybe you should take a break from the blog for a while."

Huh?

"Why would I do that?" I ask with a frown.

"Because you obviously have a lot going on, with Sophie and Brynna being home and everything." He shrugs like this makes perfect sense to him.

"I love my blog. I love to read. The authors depend on me to help them promote their books, and write reviews, and I don't want to take a break from it."

"I'm not saying you should give it up altogether. Maybe just slow down. It takes up a lot of your time."

"Are you saying that you don't want me to keep doing the blog, Isaac?" I put my silverware down and stare at him. He's never voiced this to me before. He's always seemed to be so proud of me.

What the hell?

"No," he frowns at me. "Jesus, I'm not an asshole. If you love it, keep doing it. The doctor said your headaches are caused by stress, and I'm just trying to think of ways to reduce your stress."

And I'm deliberately trying to start a fight. Great way to re-duce stress. I take another drink of water and pull in a deep breath.

"Well, I don't think the blog is stressing me out," I reply calmly.

"Okay." He finishes his pasta and pushes his plate away, watching me closely. "Is anything else going on?"

I shake my head and purse my lips. "No."

He tilts his head, those ice-blue eyes watching me closely. "If you say so."

"Did your mom call you today?" I ask, changing the subject as I rise and clear the table.

"No, what's up?" He stands to help me and we make quick work of tossing the take-out boxes and loading the dishwasher.

"We're having Christmas Eve dinner at Luke and Nat's this year, since they have a bigger living space for all of us." I turn around and lean against the kitchen counter, and smile as Isaac lifts Sophie from her bouncy seat and kisses her little cheek, whispering in her ear, making her giggle.

He is such a good dad. I have to grip the countertops at either side of my hips so I don't unconsciously rub my hand over my stomach.

The Montgomery's usually all gather together for both Christmas Eve and Christmas Day, but we exchange gifts on Christmas Eve, and I'm so damn glad because I don't think I could wait another twelve hours this year.

Not to mention, this way the three of us can have our own private Christmas morning here in our home together.

"Oh, okay. That works. Are you and I exchanging presents there or are we going to wait until Christmas morning here?" He nibbles on Sophie's fingers, making her laugh some more. "Should we make mommy wait for her Christmas presents, peach?"

"I'd like to give you one gift there, and we can do the rest here the next morning," I murmur and his eyes find mine, his head tilting again in thought at the tone of my voice.

"Are you sure you're okay?"

"I'm fine, don't be a nag, dear," I reply sarcastically.

"See, there's that mouth again. Santa can still return all those prettily wrapped presents under the tree, babe."

I grin sweetly. "I love you." I bat my eyelashes playfully and Isaac laughs, causing Sophie to laugh too.

"Mommy pretends to be a good girl, but she's naughty, Soph. Don't let her fool you." He kisses her cheek again and smiles over at me. "Come here."

"What?"

"Just come here."

I walk over to my two favorite people and he drapes an arm around me, plants his hand at the small of my back and pulls me in for a kiss.

"This is the best Christmas present, right here," he whispers against my mouth. "Just being with my girls."

Oh, I think that what I have for you comes close. I grin up at him and kiss Sophie's soft cheek.

"It's going to be a great Christmas," I murmur.

Epilogue

I squeeze Stacy's small, smooth hand in mine and kiss her fingers before I leave her with Sophie and join Caleb by the Christmas tree. I nudge my brother's shoulder and offer him a beer and follow his gaze up the tall evergreen parked in Luke and Nat's living room.

"Dude, who decorated this tree?" Caleb asks Luke, looking up at the tallest Christmas tree any of us have ever seen in a private home. Luke and Nat went all out on the décor; the huge tree climbs all the way to the cathedral ceiling, and is brightly lit with multi-colored lights and draped in bulbs and garland and tinsel. It's massive. Lights are hung outside as well, and garland with white lights is draped around the entire living space.

It looks like Santa is going to walk through the front door at any moment, kick off his big black boots, and cop a squat in a chair by the fireplace.

"We had it professionally done. There's no way in hell Nat's getting on a ladder, pregnant or not." He rubs her belly and kisses her cheek, making her blush.

We're all gathered here again, the same crew as at Thanksgiving, adding my brother Caleb who just got back from a mission in God knows where, Brynna and the girls, and Brynna's parents.

There's a hell of a lot of us.

Brynna and Matt have their heads together at the kitchen table, talking seriously and quietly, most likely about whatever in the hell the situation was that made her run from Chicago. Matt shakes his head and Brynna slams her fist on the table in frustration and then stomps away from the table.

Caleb's head snaps up at the loud sound, and he watches Brynna leave the room, his eyes narrowed and trained on her curvy ass.

Fuck, I'm not getting mixed up in it.

Stacy is sitting in the rocker with Sophie, cooing and laughing at our sweet baby. God, I go all soft when I see them, all soft skin and auburn hair – I swear, Soph's hair is going to be auburn like Stacy's. I wander over to them, hand the hot apple cider in my hand to Stacy and lift them both, sit in the chair, and settle them on my lap.

"Wow, Uncle 'saac is strong! He lifted two people!" Josie exclaims, her sweet dark eyes wide, and I chuckle.

"He is," Stacey responds and kisses my cheek. Mmm… she smells good. I bury my face in her neck and take a deep breath.

"Let's go home," I whisper in her ear, smiling as she shivers.

"We just got here," she giggles and pushes me playfully away.

"I don't care."

"Get your nose out of the poor girl's ear, Isaac. She'll go deaf." Jules is glaring at us, so I decide to taunt her. I am, after all, her big brother. It's my job.

"Nat?" I ask, not taking my eyes off my gorgeous wife.

"Yeah?" I can hear her smile.

"Take Sophie for a sec?"

"Sure."

Sophie is lifted out of our lap and I fold Stace into my arms and look into her sexy hazel eyes. They're glowing, in that way they do when she's turned on, and it makes my cock twitch. She gives me a sassy little smirk.

"You love pissing Jules off, don't you?" she whispers.

I just grin and kiss her, deeply, teasing her lips with my own, dip my tongue in her mouth, and then pull back, kiss her nose and her forehead and settle her against my chest.

"Puke," Jules mutters.

"What is it with you and PDA?" Brynna asks, walking back into the room from the deck. Matt's on the phone in the kitchen, in the middle of a heated discussion, eyes on Brynna.

I wonder if something's going on there?

But then Bryn glances at Caleb and flushes pink when he catches her gaze and offers her a grin.

I'm so not getting mixed into that. No fucking way.

"I don't mind PDA if I'm the one receiving it," Jules responds casually. "I just don't need to see my family doing it."

"Prude," Nat murmurs and kisses Sophie on the cheek.

"Don't be a bitch, Nat." Jules responds.

Natalie sticks her tongue out at her and everyone chuckles.

"How have you been feeling, Stacy?" my mom asks from the floor, where she's coloring with the twins. "Isaac mentioned that you'd been having headaches."

Stacy tenses in my arms, and I feel her inhale sharply.

What the fuck?

"Oh," she nuzzles my chest with her cheek. "I'm fine. No headaches for a few days now."

"Good." Mom nods and goes back to the girls, but I'm not buying it. I grasp Stacy's chin with my thumb and forefinger and tilt her head back to look at me. She looks a bit apprehensive and bites her delicious bottom lip.

"What?" she asks.

"You and I need to talk," I mutter and kiss her again.

"Oh, we'll talk," she mutters under her breath.

Before I can pick her up and carry her out of the room to demand some answers, dinner is served by the catering crew that Luke hired. He decided, and I agreed, that cooking for this many people was too much to ask of any of our women. They should enjoy the holiday too, so from here on out, family gatherings will be catered.

Except barbeques in the summer because my dad would have a stroke if he didn't man the grill himself.

And I can't blame him.

Dinner brings more chaos of brothers ragging on each other and stealing each other's food, kids spilling drinks, and women discussing shopping, spa treatments, movies and fashion. At least, that's what our women discuss because the whole lot of them are girly girls, and honestly, I wouldn't have them any other way.

Stacy smiles sweetly up at me as I pass her another roll. She likes to dip the bread in her gravy. Fuck, I'll give her any damn thing she wants. I may not be Luke Williams wealthy, but my girls will never want for anything.

"Stacy, would you like a glass of wine?" Jules asks. "I brought your favorite."

"Oh, um," she pauses and wipes her mouth with her green napkin. "No, thanks. I'll take some more hot cider, though."

"No wine?" I ask.

She shakes her head.

Huh.

Finally, dinner is done, and everyone moves into the living area to exchange gifts and relax. My mom grabs Soph and settles into the rocker Stacy and I vacated earlier.

I'm so excited for this. I was going to wait to give Stace this gift tomorrow morning at home, for our first Christmas as a family, but I just can't wait.

"Okay, so, I'm the oldest, so I get to give my gift first," I announce to the room.

"Yeah, you better go first, old man, 'cause in about ten minutes you'll forget what holiday this is," Will quips, earning a high-five from Caleb. I glare at them and pull a small box, wrapped in gold with a cream bow, out from under the tree and hand it to my wife.

"We didn't bring this from home," she says with a smile on her pretty lips as she looks down at it.

"Nope," I respond. "Open it."

She gently pulls the ribbon off the box, and begins to ever so fucking carefully pull the tape off the sides.

"For God's sake, woman, just open it," I growl at her, making her laugh. She knows I hate it when she does this.

"I like the paper," she murmurs.

"I'll buy you a whole roll of the shit, open the damn thing!" Will yells from across the room, stuffing more pumpkin pie in his mouth.

"Jesus, man, didn't you just have two pieces of that?" Caleb asks him.

"Shut up. Christmas." He mumbles from around the food.

"Don't talk with your mouth full!" Mom yells at him, and Stacy and I laugh with each other.

Yep, it's a Montgomery Christmas.

"Open it," I whisper.

She pulls the paper off and frowns at the soft blue Tiffany box. "Tiffany?" she asks.

"He's got good taste," Natalie boasts.

"Yes, he does," Stacy murmurs and opens the box. Inside is a platinum pendant and chain. The pendant is in the shape of a heart.

She pulls it out and smiles softly.

"Turn it over."

"What is this?"

"What is it?" Samantha asks. The girls are all straining their necks to see.

"It's Sophie's fingerprint."

Stacy's hazel eyes meet mine as they fill with tears. "This is her fingerprint?"

"Oh, what a lovely gift," Luke's mom sighs.

"Yeah, I thought you'd like to always have a piece of her with you, even if she's not with you." I shrug, feeling kind of silly, but she gives me that wide, special smile and I know that she loves it.

"It's wonderful! Thank you."

"Here, Stace," Nat hands Stacy a box wrapped in silver with a blue bow. It's the size of a small shirt box.

"We didn't bring this from home either."

"No, we didn't." She fidgets, not looking me in the eye, and looks suddenly very nervous.

"Do I get to open it?" I ask dryly.

She glances nervously around the room. Brynna gives her a discreet thumbs up and Natalie smiles brightly at her, and now I'm dying to know what's in this damn box.

"Maybe we should wait until we're home."

"Oh hell no!" Caleb and Luke yell out together. There are moans and boos, and she winces and looks back up at me, biting her lower lip.

"Hey," I cup her face in my hands and smile down at this amazing woman that I'm lucky enough to call mine. "It's okay. Whatever it is, I'll love it."

She swallows hard and whispers so low I can barely hear it, "I hope so."

She hands me the box and, because I'm a smart ass, I start to slowly unwrap it the way she always does and she giggles.

"Unless you want to die, speed it up, brother," Caleb growls.

I make quick work of the bow and paper and open the lid.

And my world stops.

It's a black and white photo of Sophie. She's sitting up on a hardwood floor with Christmas lights all around her. She has a Santa hat on that's just a little too big. Her big eyes are laughing happily at the camera. But propped up next to her is a piece of paper, and on it are the words:

I'm going to be a big sister. Merry Christmas!

My eyes shoot to Stacy's and she's got tears flowing down her cheeks.

"What?" I breathe.

She just nods.

I shake my head and look at the photo again and feel my own eyes fill. We're having another baby? *Now?*

But how?

"But…"

"I know, it's soon, but the doctor confirmed it the other day."

"Is this…?" I don't even have to finish my question before she's nodding frantically.

"Yes."

"Oh my God." I look up at our family, all staring at us with a mixture of curiosity and wonder. Brynna is crying – of course she already knew – and Natalie is rubbing her own belly serenely. "We're having another baby!"

"Holy shit, I'm getting the beer!" Will runs for the kitchen for the celebratory beer and everyone else rushes around us, pulling us into hugs, slapping me on the back. It's a blur of smiles and tears and hands and hugs.

Finally my wife is back in my arms and I'm kissing her with all I have. Jules doesn't even dare say anything about this public display of affection.

I pull back, and wipe her tears off her cheeks with my thumbs. My God, after all these years of praying and hoping and trying so fucking hard to add to our family, it's finally happening.

"I love you," she whispers in her sweet soft voice.

I bury my face in her neck, breathe in her sweet Stacy scent and murmur, "God, I love you too. Merry Christmas."

THE END

Acknowledgements:

To my Naughty Mafia: Kelli Maine, Michelle Valentine, Katie Ashley, Emily Snow and Ava Black. Your continued friendship and support is amazing. You are all so very talented. I am honored to be a part of this group. Thank you.

Lori Francis: As always, you rock. I can't thank you enough for your friendship. Love you, girl.

Tanya Robo: I love you.

To the best beta readers ever: Nichole Boyovich, Niccole Owens and Kara Erickson. You always give me the best feedback!

Kit Redeker: Thank you for taking the time to edit and offer advice. But most of all, thank you for being a mentor to me for more than ten years. You are wonderful.

To the dozens of bloggers and reviewers who have become such an amazing foundation of support and friendship. Thank you for being so welcoming!

And, as always, to the readers: I honestly don't have the words to express my gratitude. Thank you for your unending notes of love and support. I hope you enjoy Isaac and Stacy.

Happy Reading!

The WITH ME IN SEATTLE series continues in Book Two, FIGHT WITH ME, Jules and Nate's story. This book is available now.

As a special treat, here is an exclusive look at the prologue of FIGHT WITH ME...

*Please note; this is not the final version. Content may change in final editing.

Prologue

Summer

My back hits the wall with a light thud, and Nate's face is buried in my throat, his hands on my ass, skirt hiked up around my waist, pulling me up so he can cradle his still-covered erection in the apex of my thighs. I pull the hair-tie out of his thick, inky black hair and run my hands through it, holding on to him. I've never seen his hair down before; he always ties it back at the nape of his neck, and it's so sexy. It falls just above his shoulders, framing that impossibly handsome face of his that makes my insides quiver and my mouth go dry every time he looks at me.

But he's never looked at me the way he is right now, in the semi-dark hallway, in the middle of his apartment, just outside his bedroom. His gray eyes are burning as he rocks his pelvis against mine.

"Do you know how beautiful you are, Julianne," he murmurs. "I need you naked, now." He picks me up, hands still braced on my ass, and I wrap myself around him. He carries me into his bedroom, and I'm suddenly standing before him, and we are a tangle of arms and greedy hands, pulling and grasping clothes, flinging them haphazardly about the room. He doesn't turn the lights on, so I can't see him anymore, but oh, those hands. I don't know how many times I've sat in a meeting, watching these beautiful, large hands, and now they're on me.

Everywhere.

His mouth is on mine, his hands in my blonde hair, and he's kissing me with a fervor that makes my knees week. He's a really good kisser. Excellent.

Fucking amazing.

He picks me up again, cradling me in his arms this time and lays me down on the bed. The sheets are soft and cool against my naked backside, and I wish I could see him in all his naked glory. I've been daydreaming about a naked Nate since he became my boss almost a year ago. I have a feeling there is a fine, fine body lurking under all those expertly tailored business suits.

Nate follows me onto the bed, and I run my hands up his stomach, over his chest, and up to his shoulders.

Holy fuck, he's built, and his skin is warm and smooth and … *oh my.* His hands are cradling my face, kissing me tenderly now, biting and nibbling my lips, and then he leans on one elbow at the side of my head and sends his other hand down my neck, over my breast, teasing the taut nipple with his fingers, and farther south, slowly finding his target.

"Oh, God." My body bows off the soft sheets as he slips two fingers into my pussy, and his thumb gently circles my clitoris.

"Oh, you are so wet. And so fucking tight. Jesus, how long has it been for you honey?"

Really? He wants to know this now?

"Longer than I care to think about," I respond and lift my hips up into his hand. *Oh, God, what this man can do with his hands!*

"Shit, I want you. I've wanted you since I first laid eyes on you." His lips find mine, demanding and probing, licking and sucking, his tongue mirroring what his delicious fingers are doing down south, and I'm completely swept away. I've wanted him just as long.

"We shouldn't do this," I whisper unconvincingly.

"Why not?" He whispers back.

"Because… Oh, God, yes right there." My hips are circling and I skim my hands down to his ass. His hard, muscular, oh-so-sexy ass.

"You were saying?" He's nibbling down my neck.

"We could both be fired. No frat policy."

"I don't give a fuck about anyone's policy right now." His lips close over my nipple, and I lose all conscious thought. Nate licks and sucks his way down my belly, paying close attention to my navel, before heading farther south, kissing my freshly waxed – thank God! – pubis and finally planting that tongue right *there.*

"Fuck!" My hips buck up off the bed and I feel him grin before he pulls his fingers out of me, spreads my thighs wider and kisses me, deeply, his tongue pushing and swirling through my folds and inside me. I push my fingers into that glorious thick hair and hang on, and when I think I just can't take any more, he licks up to my clit and pushes a finger inside me, making a "come here" motion and I come undone, shuddering and digging my heels into the mattress, pushing my pussy against Nate's skilled mouth.

As I surface back to Planet Earth, I hear Nate rip open a foil packet and he is kissing his way back up my body, sucking on each nipple, and then kisses me. I can taste myself on his lips and I moan, wrapping my legs around his hips, lifting my pelvis, ready for him to fill me, but he doesn't. He's just braced on his hands above me, his cock cradled between my thighs. His breathing is ragged, and I wish with all my might that we'd turned on the lights so I can see his gray eyes.

"Nate, I want you."

"I know."

"Now, damnit."

"You are so fucking hot," he whispers and lowers himself to brush his lips on my forehead.

"Inside me." I reach between us and grab his erection. *Holy hell, he's hung.* He's hard and smooth, and he hasn't rolled the condom on yet. I pull up the length of him, to the tip, and …

"Holy, shit, what is that?"

He chuckles, and leans down to gently kiss me. "It's an apa," he whispers.

There is a metal bar with two small balls, one at the top and one on the underside, in the end of his penis, and I'm completely thrown. Nate, my suit-wearing, conservative-looking except for the long hair thing boss has his *penis pierced*?

"A what-a?" My fingers trace it, and then I run my forefinger around the tip of him and he sucks in a breath through his teeth.

"An apadravya. Fuck, honey."

"Why would you get this?" I ask, unexpectedly turned on and curious. *I wish I could see it!*

"You're about to find out." I hear the smile in his voice and then feel him reach between us and roll the condom down his impressive length. He kisses me again, more urgently, and buries his hands in my blonde hair. I raise my hips and feel the tip – *and those metal balls* –– at my entrance, and he slowly, oh so slowly, eases inside me.

Oh. My. God.

I can feel the metal rub against the walls of my vagina, all the way deep inside me, and he stops, buried in me, his mouth continuing to move over my own.

"Fuck, I love how tight you are." His words make me squeeze him, and hold him, my legs wrapped around his lean hips, hands in that glorious hair.

He starts to move his hips, sliding in and out of me, and the sensation is unlike any I've ever known. I feel the metal, his impressive cock, his mouth is doing crazy things to mine, and I feel my body quicken as a thin coat of sweat covers me. He picks up the pace, and rotates his hips, just enough to make me completely lose my mind.

"Come on honey, let go." And I do, violently. I cry out as Nate pushes into me, harder, once and twice, and then succumbs to his own release.

"Oh, Fuck!"

***

I just fucked my boss.

Nate pulls out of me and pulls the condom off, then tosses it on the floor beside the bed.

"Are you okay?" he asks.

No. "Yes."

"Do you need anything?" He runs his fingers down my cheek, and I again wish that the lights were on, yet I don't because I'm now feeling shy, and I never feel shy. His voice is distant, like he doesn't quite know what to do with me now, and to be honest, I don't know what to do with me either.

"No, thank you."

Oh, God, what did I just do? I just had to have the most mind-blowingly fantastic sex of my life with the one man in the world that I just can't have. When he asked me to join him for a drink here at his place after dinner out with colleagues, I should have said no, but I couldn't. I've wanted to get my hands on him from day one, but our company has a very strict no fraternization policy, and I've had a long-standing policy of my own: no fucking co-workers.

And yet, here I am, blissfully sated, and not just a little ashamed in my sexy boss's bed in his swanky thirty-floor apartment.

Fuck.

"Do you want me to turn the lights on?" Nate asks and starts to move away from me, but I put my hand out, gripping his arm to stop him.

"No, it's fine."

"You don't sound like yourself. Are you sure you're okay?"

"I'm fine. Tired, probably too much wine." Those two glasses that I sipped while drinking in Nate's deliciousness have definitely not affected my head, but it's the only excuse I have. We're acting weird with each other now, and I hate it. I don't know what I expected, I don't know him that well. He's always been professional and polite, and until tonight I had no idea that he found me the least bit attractive.

He's got a very convincing poker face.

Nate kisses my forehead and pulls the covers over us, then turns me away from him and curls up behind me.

"Go to sleep. We'll talk in the morning."

Talk? Talk about what?

I don't answer, I just lie still and wait until his breathing evens out, then wait another ten minutes to make sure he's asleep. I carefully slip out from under his heavy arm – Jeez, he's muscular! Those suits he wears are very deceiving. I fumble my way to the wall, praying I don't trip and fall on my ass, waking him up and follow it to the doorway. Turning on the hall light, I gather my clothes quickly and dress, grab my purse from Nate's large, professionally decorated, gorgeous living room, and leave.

I call a cab from the lobby of the prestigious downtown Seattle condo building and wait for my ride back to the parking garage of our office building so I can get my own car.

When I finally get home to the house I share on Alki Beach with my best friend, Natalie, I see a strange Lexus convertible in the driveway and lights coming from the kitchen at the back of the house.

"Natalie?"

"In the kitchen!"

"Do you have company?" I am so not in the mood to meet Nat's new friend.

"Yeah," she calls back.

"I'll see you tomorrow, I'm going to bed." I climb the stairs to my bedroom, closing the door behind me and take a long, hot shower. My skin is still sensitive from my romp in Nate's bed, and his scent clings to me, all clean and musky and sexy, and I can't help but regret leaving just a little. Perhaps there could have been more fun during the night before the harsh light of day settled in.

And along with it, The Talk.

No, thank you.

I really don't need to have Nate spell out all the reasons why this was a one night indiscretion. I certainly don't think I can handle the awkwardness of the morning after. It's better to just pretend like it never happened, and get back to business as usual.

I pull on pink panties and a white cami and pull my phone out of my purse on my way to bed. There are no messages or texts.

He's probably as relieved I left as I am.

I lie awake all night, trying to figure out what I'm going to say when I call in sick at work tomorrow.